Outrageously
Alice

Books by Phyllis Reynolds Naylor

Outrageously Alice

Phyllis Reynolds Naylor

A Jean Karl Book

Atheneum Books for Young Readers

Atheneum Books for Young Readers
An imprint of Simon & Schuster
Children's Publishing Division
1230 Avenue of the Americas
New York, New York 10020
Text copyright © 1997 by Phyllis Reynolds Naylor
Book design by Ethan Trask
The text of this book is set in Berkeley Book Old Style.
First Edition
Printed in the United States of America
10 9 8 7 6 5 4 3 2 1
Library of Congress Cataloging-in-Publication Data
Naylor, Phyllis Reynolds.
Outrageously Alice / Phyllis Reynolds Naylor.—1st ed.
p. cm.
Summary: Alice is in the eighth grade, and while she wants her life
to be exciting and outrageous, she also wants to feel protected and safe.
ISBN 0-689-80354-0
[1. Schools—Fiction. 2. Identity—Fiction. 3. Single-parent family—Fiction.
4. Family life—Fiction.] I. Title.
PZ7.N24Ou   1997
[Fic]—dc20   96-7744

To Erinn Lindsay Geyer,

whose love of books will make them

her lifelong friends

Contents

Outrageously
Alice

Facing Up

A bout the third week of October, I decided it was turning out to be one of the weirdest months of my life. Not that there have been that many of them—Octobers, I mean. Thirteen, to be exact. But here's what had happened so far:

Lester, my twenty-one-year-old brother, who has been juggling two or more girlfriends for several years, just got word that one of his *main* girlfriends, Crystal, was engaged to be married at Thanksgiving. And I was to be a bridesmaid. Now that's weird.

And of course I was still holding my breath to see whether Miss Summers, my English teacher last year, would marry Dad or our vice principal, Mr. Sorringer, who's in love with her, too.

Then Elizabeth, my friend who lives across the street, got a baby brother. At last she found out what a boy looks like naked. Is *that* weird, or what?

And finally, the student council at our junior high voted to create a haunted house for Halloween in the school gym to raise money for our library. What the school was going to do, see, was charge a buck fifty apiece to scare little kids half out of their minds. Patrick, my boyfriend, who's vice president of the student council, asked if I wanted to help out.

Well, why not? I thought. October couldn't get any crazier than it was already.

I was wrong. It got even crazier. Crystal Harkins's maid of honor invited me to a bridal shower—a *lingerie* shower—and I'd never been to a shower before.

But you know what? All of these things—the engagement, the bridal shower, the baby brother, the haunted house—were happening to somebody else. I was just on the outside looking in. Not much that is really dramatic, outrageous, and wonderful has ever happened to *me*—something to remember forever and ever. If there was a prize for the girl with the most boring life, I thought, I'd win it, hands down.

Here's where I miss my mom. If Mom were alive, she could have told me how to keep from being ordinary. She'd know what you take to a bridal shower, too. But because she died when I was four, I have to ask Dad and Lester, who don't know diddly, all my questions, and if I'm really desperate, I call Aunt Sally in Chicago. This time I tried Dad and Lester first.

"I've been invited to a lingerie shower for Crystal," I said at dinner that night. "Any ideas about what I could get her?"

"A chastity belt," Lester mumbled.

"What?"

"He's joking, Al," said Dad. He and Lester call me Al.

Lester just glared down at his tuna and noodles. I guess he figured his girlfriends would go on waiting all their lives

2

for him to make up his mind, and it was really a shock that one of them got engaged.

"What *is* a chastity belt?" I asked, curious.

"A metal device that some medieval men bought their wives when the men were going to be gone from their fiefdoms," said Dad. "Only the husbands had the key. It was to insure that their wives would be faithful while they were away. Now you know how ridiculous this conversation is getting to be."

I couldn't believe it. "You mean it fit around their . . . ?"

"Exactly," said Lester. "Now shut up."

"But how did they go to the bathroom?" I have to know things like that.

"With difficulty, I imagine," Dad said.

I looked from Dad to Lester. That was so unfair! "What about the *men?* Did *they* have to wear chastity belts while they were gone to make sure *they* weren't unfaithful?" I demanded.

Lester winced.

I was indignant. "What about a metal pipe that fitted over their . . . ?"

"Okay, okay! Just drop it, will you?" Lester snapped.

He's been pretty touchy these days. Ever since Crystal returned all the things he'd ever given her and told us she was getting married, he's been a real grouch.

I'm not sure why I was asked to be one of her bridesmaids, but I think it's because her fiancé's younger brother is going to be in the wedding party. He's seventeen, and Crystal needs someone young to walk back up the aisle

with him. Or maybe Crystal's still mad at Lester and is trying to rub it in. Whatever, I'm prepared to enjoy myself.

"I don't see how you can buy Crystal anything without
knowing her sizes," Dad said, trying to be helpful.

"Big," said Lester. "Big hips, big boobs—a narrow waist,
though."

"Do *you* want to buy it for me, Lester?" I asked.

He glared daggers at me. "What do *you* think?"

I went up to my room after dinner and tried to figure out
what would look nice on Crystal Harkins. If she were to
step out of the bathroom on her wedding night and present
herself to her new husband, what would look best on her?
She has short red hair in a feather cut, and I imagined her
in a sheer white nightgown with lace over her breasts so you
could see her nipples.

I took the invitation out of the envelope again to see if
they gave Crystal's sizes on the back. They didn't. But there
was a little card enclosed that said the shower was being
given jointly by Betsy Hall, Crystal's maid of honor, and
Fantasy Creations, which, it said, for eleven years has been
making the kind of lingerie "every woman dreams of possessing, but only a few will dare."

"Huh?" I said.

I went straight to the phone and dialed my cousin Carol
in Chicago. She's Aunt Sally's daughter, and I always try her
first. Carol's a couple years older than Lester and, having
been married once to a sailor, she knows everything there is
to know in the sex department. The phone rang eight times

4

at her place, though, and she didn't answer, so I had to call Aunt Sally.

"Is Carol there, by chance?" I asked when Uncle Milt answered.

"Why, Alice, sweetheart! How nice to hear from you!" he said. "No, she's on a business trip, but your aunt Sally's right here. Just a minute."

"Alice?" said Aunt Sally. "What's wrong?"

I come from one of those families where if you call long distance, they figure someone just died.

"Nothing! I just wanted to ask a question."

"Oh! Certainly!" said Aunt Sally, sounding relieved. She's Mom's older sister, who took care of us for a while after Mom died, before we moved to Maryland.

"I've been invited to a bridal shower, and I'm wondering what to buy."

"Not Pamela or Elizabeth!" Aunt Sally gasped. Pamela's my other best friend, and we'd all three gone by Amtrak to visit Aunt Sally last June.

"No. An old girlfriend of Lester's, actually. She's marrying someone else."

"Good for her!" said Aunt Sally, who thinks it's time Lester settled down himself. "Now what kind of shower is it to be? Kitchen? Linen?"

"Lingerie," I said. "The kind every woman dreams of possessing, but only a few will dare."

There was a soft noise at the other end of the line. I think Aunt Sally had just sat down.

"Pajamas," she said finally. "Alice, you can't go wrong with pajamas. If I were you, I'd buy a pretty pair of pink pajamas, and I promise she'll thank you."

Crystal would thank me, all right, but would she wear them? I thought not. So after I'd talked to Aunt Sally, I dialed the maid of honor herself, who told me that I wasn't supposed to buy anything in advance.

"Just come," Betsy said, "and you can order from the Fantasy Creations catalog when you get here. We'll have Crystal's sizes, and she'll choose the things she likes. You might like to buy something for yourself, too."

Now *that* was the weirdest idea of all, because I don't have much of a body yet. I suppose that will come. At least I hope so. But what I really want is a life, not a new bra. I want to do things. I want people to notice me.

Elizabeth Price is beautiful, she takes ballet and piano, and she has a little brother to take care of, even though his poop is yellow and Elizabeth says she'll never eat mustard again. Gorgeous Pamela Jones, my other best friend, is taking tap and gymnastics, and Patrick's on the track team, the debate team, the student council, and the school newspaper. He's also in the band. Me? I'm just not a joiner, I guess.

When Patrick came over later, we walked to our old elementary school and fooled around on the jungle gym. He chased me over and under the bars but never did tag me, and finally we sat on the swings, turning around and around until the chains wouldn't wind anymore, and then we'd let go and spin the other way.

Patrick was talking about how busy he was going to be this year, with track meets and all, and suddenly I said, "Patrick, is it possible to get through life without joining anything?"

"You mean . . . like a church or a political party?"

"A band, a chorus, a club, a group, Girl Scouts, Boy Scouts, Triple A, *anything*?"

Patrick dug his feet in the ground to stop the swing. "I suppose, but why would you want to? You allergic to people?"

"No! I like people! I just don't want to end up being like everybody else. Like a . . . a piano key, that's all." I thought that was pretty original, but Patrick thought I was nuts.

"Well, I guess you can have a full and interesting life without joining anything, but what *do* you do for excitement, Alice? Besides me, of course." He grinned.

Suddenly it seemed like one of the most embarrassing questions I'd ever been asked.

"I guess I figured I was busy enough," I murmured.

"A college might not think so," said Patrick.

"What does college have to do with it?"

"You have to list all your hobbies and extracurricular activities on your application, Mom says. And if you don't *have* any, well . . ."

I don't know how Patrick could even stand to kiss me later. I was a zip, a zero, a zed, a zilch. If someone were to take my pulse, I'll bet I wouldn't have one.

I marched straight upstairs to Lester's room, where he

was working on his senior philosophy paper, and burst through the door. "I need a life!" I bellowed.

Lester jumped a foot. "Good grief, Al! *Knock* first! You want to see cardiac arrest?"

"Lester," I wailed. "I have no body, no personality, no hobbies! I've got to join something quick. What should it be?"

"The army," said Lester. "Now scram."

I went downstairs to talk to Dad, but he'd gone out for the evening, so I lay on my stomach on the sofa, turning the pages of our school newspaper there on the floor, looking at photos of girls who had bodies *and* lives—cheerleaders, basketball players, singers, skaters . . .

On the last page, along with the ads for Hamburger Hamlet, Pizza Hut, Putt-Putt Golf, and Cineplex Theaters, was a boxed announcement:

JOIN THE CROWD! JOIN THE FUN!

Students: It's still not too late to join a club. Get the most out of your junior high experience. Don't let another week slip by without signing up for something extra. These clubs need new members:

Debate Team	*Girls' Soccer*
French Club	*Science Club*
Camera Club	*Explorers' Club*

I checked numbers three and six, tore out the ad, and stuck it in my notebook.

Getting a Life

I resolved when I got up the next morning that by the time I came home again, I'd have a life. As soon as I got to school, I stopped by the office and signed up for both the Camera Club and the Explorers' Club. It wasn't as though I were signing away all my worldly goods, I told myself. I could leave any time.

"You did *what?*" Elizabeth asked me in Mr. Everett's health class.

"I just wanted to try something different," I said.

"I'll bet they're full of dorks," Pamela commented. She was wearing a red sweater with a Wonderbra beneath. *Must* have, because her breasts were rounder and higher than usual. Pamela not only has breasts, she flaunts them. "I looked over that sign-up sheet," she went on, as Mr. Everett walked in the room and took attendance, "and you know what the motto of the Explorers' Club is? 'The world is our province.' Oh, brother!"

I thought about that a minute. Mr. Everett tapped for attention, but I whispered, "I think it just means that almost everywhere is interesting—that we're not limited. Whatever, I want to see what it's like."

"We're all doing different things this year!" Elizabeth complained. "Not a single one of us has signed up for the same activity."

"Miss Price, *if* you please!" said Mr. Everett.

Elizabeth blushed and faced forward, and Mr. Everett began the class.

I was surprised, frankly, that that could even happen. Elizabeth's usually on the edge of her seat waiting for Mr. Everett to enter the room. She's had a crush on him since the first day of school. Our health teacher is six foot six and looks like Robert Redford's kid brother. Robert Redford's son! Elizabeth told us once that she loves him so much, it hurts. Hurts, I suppose, because she can't have him. I can understand that. I've felt that way about Mom. Which is why I want so much for Dad to marry Miss Summers. But Lester says that's not reason enough for people to marry, and I suppose he's right.

It turned out that the Camera Club met every two weeks, and wouldn't be meeting again until Tuesday of the week after next, but the Explorers' Club was that same day after school. So I told Elizabeth and Pamela to go home without me and I'd catch a city bus later.

I should have known, I guess, when I discovered that the Explorers' Club met in my old world studies classroom, that it was going to be a glorified geography lesson.

That there were only six kids there should have been Clue Number Two. The faculty sponsor sat at the back of the room grading papers, as though she couldn't care less.

As soon as I'd been introduced, the guy in charge said that when they'd met last time, they'd decided that this week each would tell the most interesting place they'd ever visited and any problems they'd encountered. That was when I should have slipped out. Because the farthest west I've ever been is Chicago, and the farthest east is Ocean City, and after listening to the other kids tell about a trip to India with an aunt, or Antarctica with their dad, all I had to report was a visit to Aunt Sally on Amtrak.

"Well," somebody said charitably, "what was the most interesting thing that happened on that trip, then?"

I was about to tell them how a man had made a pass at Pamela, but then I realized that was her story to tell, not mine. Here I was again, living my life through other people. So instead of telling them about that trip, I told them about the very first time I'd gone to Chicago on the train, and when I'd tried to get up in the middle of the night to use the john, the bed came down on my head.

There was silence so long and profound that when someone laughed at last, I knew it was only to put me out of my misery. I decided to walk home through the leaves instead of taking the bus, and realized just how disappointed I was. I'd thought we might go prowling around Washington and

Maryland or something—explore the tunnels under the Lincoln Memorial, or hike along the C&O Canal. No, someone had told me, it was more like a travel club. So much for the Explorers' Club.

I thought about myself and where exactly I was headed. It wasn't that I was unhappy. But the more I examined my life, the more it seemed to consist of getting up, going to school, seeing my friends, going to bed, getting up, going to school, and—on Saturdays—working half-days at the Melody Inn. That was it.

All the things that *could* happen—like Dad eloping with Miss Summers and taking me on their honeymoon with them, or the Publishers Clearing House Prize Patrol descending on our porch, or my getting chosen most popular girl in eighth grade—nothing like that ever happened. In my thirteen years of life, in fact, when had anything happened to me that could be called remotely outrageous? Embarrassing, yes. Outrageous, no. Just once in my thirteen years, I decided, I would like something truly remarkable to happen that would make people sit up and take notice. I'm not particularly superstitious, but if it doesn't happen in your thirteenth year, I figure it's not going to happen at all. Well, there was still the Camera Club to look forward to.

Dad and Lester were already eating dinner when I came in.

"Where were you?" asked Dad. "I was beginning to worry."

I placed my books on the counter and took off my jacket. "The world," I said, "is my province."

Lester rolled his eyes. "God save the queen," he said.

That evening I got a call from Crystal Harkins. Lester answered the phone, and it was strange to hear him say, "Al, for you. It's Crystal."

If he was pining away for his old girlfriend, he never let on.

"Hello?" I said.

"Hi, Alice. I just wondered if I could drive over some evening and show you the bridesmaid dress I've picked. My aunt has already started sewing some of them."

"Sure! Come tonight if you want!" I said. It wasn't outrageous or remarkable, but it was better than another evening of homework and TV.

Lester's ears picked up like a dog's when he heard her car drive up later, and he managed to get up to his room before she rang the bell.

Crystal looked sparkly and slimmer than when I'd seen her last. I noticed she glanced around, probably looking for Lester, but she didn't mention him, so neither did I. She dropped her coat on a chair and sat down beside me on the couch. Her perfume was absolutely wonderful.

"Here's the dress I like, and I hope you do, too," she said. "I tried to pick one you could wear again; if you go to the eighth-grade dance, maybe you could wear it then."

She turned to a page in a magazine that showed a bride

attended by her bridesmaids, and the bridesmaids were all wearing jade green dresses, barebacked, with a full filmy net layer for the skirt, slit down the middle, revealing a tighter skirt of jade green satin beneath. The dress was gorgeous on the models, but I wasn't sure how it would look on me.

"It's beautiful, Crystal," I said. "But how . . ." I frowned at the picture.

"Problems?"

"The bridesmaids . . . the ones who have breasts, I mean . . . how do they wear a bra?"

"Well, Alice, you can get paste-on cups that you stick on under your breasts, and they hold them up."

I stared. "You mean, like a Band-Aid?"

"Something like that. Or you can buy a bra that fastens around the waist and there's a sort of wire framework that sticks up in front to hold the breasts in place."

"Like a chastity belt?" I asked. I don't know why, I just blurted it out.

Crystal put down the bride's magazine and stared at me. "Of course not. Where did you hear about that?"

"Forget it," I said. "Anyway, Crystal, it's gorgeous. Of course I'll wear the dress. I love it."

"Wonderful," she said. "Since my aunt's making them, you'll only have to pay fifty dollars for the material. You'll need shoes dyed to match, of course. But I'll let you know about those next week. I've brought a tape measure; we need to get your sizes, okay?"

She measured me there in the living room and after she left, I was still staring after her. Dad came out of the kitchen.

"Dad!" I cried in dismay. "Did you know we have to pay for the dress and shoes? I thought the bride paid for everything!"

"Guess we've got a lot to learn about weddings, don't we? Your mother would have known. . . ."

"But what am I going to do? I don't *have* fifty dollars. I'm lucky to have fifty cents."

"I think we can probably handle that. If it's a dress you can wear later to high school dances, maybe it's not too bad. Of course, you can't grow at all between now and your senior year, you understand." We laughed.

Crystal had made a copy of that page in the magazine and left it with me, so I called Elizabeth to come over and see the dress. She was only too glad to get out of the house.

"Nathan's howling up in his crib, and the whole place smells like diapers. It's depressing," she said. "You know, Alice, we don't really have to have children when we're grown. I mean, women can live full and complete lives even if they don't have babies, can't they?"

"I suppose," I said. "There's so much out there we don't know anything about, Elizabeth."

I guess she was already feeling shaky, and that remark didn't help. "Like what?" she asked warily.

"Paste-on bra cups, for one."

"What?"

15

"You glue them to the underside of your breasts to keep them upright if you want to wear a backless dress."

"How do you get them off?"

"Pull, I guess."

"Oh, that's so gross!"

"And then, of course, there's a chastity belt. . . ."

"What?" she cried.

"It's made of metal, and your husband locks it on you with a key when he goes on a trip to make sure you're faithful." I don't know why I do that to Elizabeth.

"What?" she screeched.

"Never mind," I said. "I'll explain it to you sometime when you're feeling strong. But remember, we don't have to get married, either."

3

Jungle Fever

On the night of the shower for Crystal, Aunt Sally called to make sure I wore a dress, which is why I ripped one pair of panty hose, put another pair on three times before I got them right, ironed a rayon dress that was handed down from my cousin Carol, and wore a string of pearls (fake, of course) that used to be my mom's, because Aunt Sally said you could never go wrong with pearls. Then, at a quarter of seven, Lester drove me to Betsy Hall's.

"Les," I asked as I sat with my legs crossed, hands over the purse in my lap, "how do you really feel about Crystal getting married?"

"Well, I think it was pretty sudden, and I just hope she knows what she's doing," he said. "I mean, one minute she was dating me, and the next she's marrying Peter."

"One minute?" I said. "Lester, sometimes two or three months went by and you'd hardly even call her."

"Hey, she can dial my number as easily as I can dial hers," he said.

"She did! A lot! But you were usually out with Marilyn."

He shrugged. "Well, that's the way the ball bounces."

I was feeling pretty grown-up and excited as I went up the steps and rang the bell. As soon as I walked inside, though, I knew I'd dressed all wrong, because every woman there was in jeans. They were good jeans, of course, designer jeans, with a nice shirt or sweater, but I looked as out of place in my rayon dress and pearls as a cream puff on a plate of bagels. Not only that, but I was definitely the youngest person present, and they all looked at me in surprise. All but Crystal.

"Alice!" she said. "I'm so glad you could come."

"This is Alice McKinley," Betsy told the others. "She's paired with Peter's younger brother in the wedding party."

Just a kid, in other words. I wished she hadn't felt she had to explain me, but the women all seemed friendly. I took a chair beside the couch and tried to scoot it back as far as I could, to be invisible.

Everyone was drinking coffee, but Betsy got a Coke for me. I was watching a pretty woman with a clipboard on her lap and a large sample case beside her chair that read FANTASY CREATIONS.

"Welcome, everybody!" she said. "I'm Joan, and the only rule tonight is to remember that you're here to have fun. I am going to help *you* make your wildest fantasies come true."

Everybody laughed.

"Not mine!" said someone, and we laughed some more.

"Okay, *some* of your fantasies, anyway," Joan said. "First, I want to thank Betsy for throwing this party and including my company, Fantasy Creations, and I know you all will join me in giving Crystal our best wishes for her marriage."

Everybody clapped and smiled.

"As you probably know, this is a different kind of shower, in which Crystal will select, and hopefully model, the lingerie of her choice."

"Now wait a minute!" cried Crystal.

More laughter and hooting.

"Here's the way we'll do it," said Joan. "After Crystal has selected the items she'd most like to receive, we'll pass the list around and you can sign up for the one you'd like to give her as your shower gift. That way you can be sure of giving the bride-to-be something you know she really wants. And remember, if you order something additional for yourself, you will get it at twenty-five percent off."

Betsy poured more coffee and brought out a plate of cookies.

"But now for the fun part," said Joan. She began passing around sheets of paper and tiny sharpened pencils. "A little quiz, ladies, and remember there aren't any right or wrong answers. Just answer honestly, and you don't have to read your answers aloud. Circle your scores as you go."

As soon as people looked at the sheets they started laughing, and I couldn't wait to see what was so funny. When Joan handed one to me, I read *Test Your Sensuality*.

All over the room I could hear murmurs and giggles. I looked at the questions:

1. Have you ever worn a flower in your hair?
   10 points
2. Are you wearing matching bra and panties?
   10 points
3. Have you ever had a sensual experience while swimming?
   15 points

I think the others were going a lot faster than I was, because there began to be loud whoops and shrieks. I was still trying to think what a sensual experience while swimming would be—certainly not the time the guys tried to toss me in the pool. So far I hadn't got any points at all. No, I thought, wait a minute. I remembered sticking a dandelion behind my ear once when I was in kindergarten, so I gave myself ten points.

4. Have you ever mentally undressed a stranger?
   20 points
5. Have you ever removed any lingerie during a meal?
   10 points

"This is a riot!" said Crystal.

"Boy, I'm glad my mother's not here," someone murmured, and that got a laugh.

What if *my* mother were here? I wondered. I think I'd

have liked her to come, just to see what *her* answers might have been. I wondered what Miss Summers's answers would be.

> 6. Have you ever taken a feather and started at the top of his nose and ended at the tip of his toes?
>   *25 points*

I could feel my face getting red. People actually *did* this stuff?

> 7. Have you ever gift wrapped yourself for your favorite male?
>   *10 points*

I couldn't believe what I was reading. Maybe I *wouldn't* want my mother here.

"A few more minutes, girls," said Joan.

> 8. Have you ever given a massage to a member of the opposite sex?
>   *20 points*
> 9. Have you ever made love in a room other than the bedroom?
>   *15 points*
> 10. Have you ever used whipped cream for anything besides dessert?
>   *25 points*

I hadn't even got used to the idea of gift wrapping myself before I had to face the fact that some people made love in the dining room. Then I had to wonder what whipped cream had to do with anything. And suddenly I imagined myself standing naked covered with whipped cream in the dining room and I sucked in my breath.

"Look at Alice!" somebody said. "Look at her blush!"

"Oh, Alice!" laughed Crystal.

"One more minute," said Joan. "Tally up your scores, now, and we'll go around the room and read them off."

I tried desperately to come up with points. Ten points for sticking a dandelion behind my ear in kindergarten. Twenty points for thinking what it would be like on my wedding night if I married Patrick and how he would look in the shower; I guess that would be mentally undressing someone, but it wasn't a stranger. I'd fudge a little on that one. Ten points for taking my socks off once during a meal (socks count as underwear, don't they?), and twenty points for giving Dad a back rub once. Well, a shoulder rub, anyway. Sixty points.

We went around the room. One hundred and twenty, one hundred and five, ninety-five, one-forty, one-ten (that was Crystal), and finally they got to me. I thought of lying, but what if we had to turn in our sheets?

"Sixty," I said, and they laughed.

"It's okay," Joan said to me, and then to the others, "You, too, were beginners once." More laughter.

"It's all in fun, Alice," Crystal said, trying to reassure me, but it just made me feel that much more self-conscious.

"To Dianne, with one hundred and forty points, a little present," said Joan, fishing in her briefcase.

"Hey, she lied!" someone called. "Boo! Hiss!"

"Hey, Dianne, what *didn't* you do?" another woman asked, to more laughter.

"For the winner," Joan said, and held up a fur bikini. Dianne shrieked and hid it in her purse.

"And for Alice," said Joan, smiling at me.

My heart sank. A chastity belt, that's what the booby prize would be. Instead, Joan handed me a tiny box, and when I opened it, I found a pair of teddy bear earrings, like a little kid would wear.

"Until she's old enough to wear a real teddy," said Joan good-naturedly, and the women clapped. All I wanted to do was crawl out the door and go home.

After that, Joan showed us all the lingerie she had in her sample case, and Crystal made a list of the ones she liked best. The list went around the room, along with the prices, and we put our names beside the ones we decided to give to Crystal, and a check mark for anything we wanted to order for ourselves. I signed up for a pair of satin tap pants for Crystal, but that was all. I tried to imagine me wearing underwear from this catalog and then having to undress in gym.

Most of the women took lingerie samples into the bathroom or bedroom to try them on, and once in a while one would come out and ask us how she looked in a black lace teddy or a long slinky gown with a slit up the side. Not me.

I was embarrassed from the moment I'd walked in the front door in my pantyhose and pearls to when Betsy came out of the bathroom in a teddy called "Jungle Fever." The other women shrieked when they saw her. It was a nylon leopard-skin print, and it had a paw print over each breast and another down by the crotch. It was cut so high at the sides that it looked as though Betsy's legs reached all the way to her armpits. And the bra part pushed her breasts up so far, I'll bet she could have rested her chin on them.

The minute the first woman picked up her shoulder bag to leave, I went to the phone and told Lester I was ready to come home. Then I said good-bye to everyone, hugged Crystal, thanked Betsy, and went out to sit on the curb.

It was one of the most beautiful October evenings I'd ever seen. The air was warm, and there was a gentle breeze that sent dry leaves scuttling along the sidewalk until it sighed itself out. A ring of gold leaves around the streetlight shone with a misty gleam. I leaned forward, head on my knees, and wished that Patrick were there with his arm around me.

Part of me wanted things to go on forever just like that— hugs and kisses and holding hands on the sidewalk at night—and the other part wanted to do something wild, like walk out of a bathroom in a "Jungle Fever" teddy. Could I ever imagine myself doing that? Right now, the answer was no.

Is this what my life would be like, then? Feeling too

scared to be outrageous and too ordinary if I didn't? I could see what was ahead for me: one opportunity after another to do something unusual, and never getting up the nerve to do it. By the time Lester pulled up at the curb, I felt childish and innocent and stupid and embarrassed and thoroughly disgusted at myself for not having a better time at the party.

As soon as I got in, I slammed the door, kicked off my pumps, wriggled out of my pantyhose, and took off my fake pearls, dropping them in my purse.

"You through, or are you just getting started?" Lester asked, wondering.

"Just go," I said sullenly.

"What kind of a party *was* this, anyway?"

"A grown-up party for sophisticated women of which I am definitely not one," I said.

He drove for a few blocks without saying anything, then tried again: "So you didn't have a very good time?"

"Let's just say it was educational."

"Oh. Crystal was there, of course. . . ."

"Of course. She's getting married, isn't she? And for the first two weeks of her married life, she will thrill her husband with a new set of lingerie each night."

"Sounds interesting," said Lester.

I felt like crying because I was so awkward and inexperienced. I wondered if it was possible that most of the women had exaggerated their answers. *I* certainly had.

"Lester . . ." I said, and was surprised to hear my voice quaver. He glanced over quickly. Lester knows when I'm about to bawl.

"If I asked you some personal questions, would you answer truthfully?" If *he* hadn't done any of that stuff, then I'll bet those women hadn't, either.

"Well, I don't know how personal you're going to get," Lester told me.

"All you have to do is say yes or no. I'm not asking for details, and I won't tell anyone. Okay?"

"Okay. Shoot."

I skipped the questions about the flower in the hair, and matching bra and panties. I hoped I could still remember the others, because I wanted Les to answer every one.

"Have you ever had a sensual experience while swimming?"

"I *always* have a sensual experience while swimming," he said. "Just looking at girls in bikinis is a sensual experience for me."

"Have you ever mentally undressed a stranger?"

"All the time."

"Have you ever massaged a member of the opposite sex?"

"Of course. You've seen me put suntan lotion on Marilyn, haven't you?"

He was probably up to sixty points already, and we had just begun.

"Have you ever gift wrapped yourself for a woman?"

"Are you nuts?"

Aha. One down. "Have you . . . let's see—ever removed your underwear during a meal?"

"Why would I want to do that?"

I was beginning to feel better all the time. They *had* lied, I'll bet.

"Have you ever taken a feather and started at the tip of a woman's nose and ended at her toes?"

Lester whistled. "That must have been some party!" he said. "What did they *do,* anyway?"

"They answered questions."

"*These* questions? You're kidding! What'd Crystal say?"

"Lester, I asked *you* a question."

"Oh. Well, no, I can't say I've used a feather, but . . . listen, Al. How many more of these?"

"Just two. Have you ever made love in any room besides the bedroom?"

"Whoaa . . . next question."

"Have you ever used whipped cream for something besides dessert?"

Les didn't answer that one, either. He just looked in my direction as he pulled in our driveway and said, "Listen, Al, promise me something: If you're ever invited to a party like that again, take me along. Okay?"

4

In the Closet

The thing about Halloween, you can be as outrageous as you want. I sure didn't want to be that ridiculous-looking girl in the rayon dress and panty hose; I wanted to be somebody with personality and pizazz!

When I put in my three hours at the Melody Inn the next morning, I told Marilyn Rawley about the haunted house in the school gym, and she asked what I'd be wearing. The Melody Inn is one of a chain of music stores, and my dad's the manager of the one in Silver Spring. Marilyn, who runs the Gift Shoppe there, is Lester's current girlfriend.

On this particular morning I was putting price stickers on some fountain pens that looked as though they were made of marble, but if you looked closer, you discovered that the long wavy lines were really the names of composers stretched from one end of the pen to the other.

"I always dressed up like a Gypsy," Marilyn told me. "In fact, it was the only thing I ever wanted to be on Halloween."

That figured, because Marilyn is sort of the barefoot type,

and if she ever marries Lester, it will probably be in a white cotton dress, standing in a field of daisies.

"I haven't decided yet," I told her. "Something that's about as far away from 'Alice' as I can get."

"What's wrong with being Alice?"

"You don't have to live with her; I do," I said.

Janice Sherman, the assistant manager, came over to ask me to help out in the sheet music department when I was through, and I asked Janice what she used to wear to Halloween parties when she was my age. To tell the truth, I can't even imagine Janice Sherman my age. I'll bet she was wearing glasses with a chain attached when she was three years old.

She surprised me, though.

"A hobo," she said. "Mother sewed patches on our clothes, and my sister and I went trick-or-treating as hoboes." You can't always tell about a person just by looking.

By the time I went home at noon, I had decided to go as a showgirl. Elizabeth, with her long dark hair, was going as Morticia from *The Addams Family,* and Pamela wore the cat costume she'd bought once for a dance recital, only she wore black tights instead of net stockings, and said I could wear the stockings.

So here's how I looked on Halloween: black suede platform shoes from Elizabeth's mother; black net stockings from Pamela; a black nylon sarong-type skirt from my cousin Carol in Chicago, which I found in a box of bathing suits she'd sent last summer; an orange jersey top from Pamela's mother; and some kind of peacock feather head-dress that Mrs. Jones wore once for Mardi Gras. Weird, I guess, was the only way to describe me, but I sure didn't look like the cupcake I'd been at Crystal's shower.

After I'd dressed, I slipped into my chair at the table for a quick bite before I left. Lester looked up, then did a double take.

"Hello, have we met?" he asked.

Dad just raised his eyebrows.

"It's the new me," I said.

"You look like a vamp," said Dad. He has a vocabulary right out of the Middle Ages.

"A pickup," Lester interpreted. "You're not actually going out like that, are you?"

"It's Halloween!" I said. "Besides, I can't believe this is the same guy who asked Marilyn Rawley to cook his birth-day dinner wearing only boots and a bikini."

"That's because I know Marilyn can behave herself. I'm not so sure about you," he said.

"Thank you, Lester, for your confidence in me," I told him, scarfing down another bite of pizza, and then I ran back upstairs to brush my teeth before I went across the street to ride with Elizabeth.

Mr. Price picked up Pamela and then Patrick on the way— Patrick was dressed like a zombie—and drove us to the school.

"Wow!" Patrick said when he saw me.

"You're pretty cool yourself," I said.

The gym looked really creepy. The pumpkin I'd carved a week too early had begun to rot, so it was just perfect to set by the ticket window, with strings of decay oozing out its eyes and nose. Someone said that a couple of smaller kids had taken one look at the pumpkin and decided they'd seen enough, but still the line of children went all the way out the front door and around to the driveway, and more kept coming all the time.

We'd figured on about two hundred kids, at a buck fifty each, which would mean three hundred dollars for our school library. The whole gym had been partitioned off into a long winding passageway, and we took turns escorting kids through it one by one. They had to stick their hands in a bowl of peeled grapes, of course, for eyeballs, and another bowl of cooked lasagna noodles, which we told them were guts, and all along the way ghosts wailed and zombies moaned and witches cackled.

Things leaped out at them, lights flashed, doors groaned, cobwebs swished, and when the kids reached the very end—or what they *thought* was the end—my job was to take each kid, one at a time, to a tiny broom closet, sit him on a stool, and tell him to wait for the others. Then Brian or Mark or whoever was taking his turn at it would start to moan at the back of the closet and snap on a flashlight, holding it just under his mask as the kid turned around. It would look for all the world like a floating head, and after the kid let out a bloodcurdling scream, I'd take him out the back door where his parents were waiting. If he was under eight years old, we'd skip the closet.

About halfway through the evening, though, a couple of parents called the school to complain. They said that the closet thing was going to give their children nightmares, so when I got the word, I opened the broom closet door and said, "Brian? Mark? Mr. Ormand says we've got to cut this out. It's scaring too many kids, okay?"

In answer, a hand clamped down on my arm, pulled me inside, and somebody put his arms around me, hugging me close to his body, and kissed me hard on the lips. Not only that, but his tongue was pushing its way into my mouth.

"Hey!" I said, backing up. "Cut it out!"

But the arms pulled me back, and the tongue kissed me again.

"Stop it!" I said, pushing away with all my strength, and I tumbled out into the hall.

I stayed at my post the rest of the evening, escorting kids through the cobwebs at the back exit and giving each one a licorice lollipop before he left, but all the while I was trying to figure out who that was in the closet. It was probably done as a joke, but still, a tongue going in and out of your mouth isn't exactly a joke.

At some point in the evening, Brian had been in there, I

knew, and possibly Mark. But there were also other eighth-grade boys I hardly knew. It could have been anyone.

The more I thought about it, the angrier I got. What if I had reached in there and unzipped a guy's trousers? Would *he* think it was a joke? At the same time, though, I was thinking that finally something outrageous had happened to me, and I didn't like it much.

When we walked over to McDonald's for cheeseburgers afterward in our costumes, I kept looking at all the guys, wondering if I could figure out who it had been. I hadn't a clue, and no one seemed to be giving me sideways glances. I wondered what would happen if I told Patrick. If he'd keep asking around till he found out who it was, then pound the guy to a pulp. Somehow I felt it would be a mistake, so I made an even bigger mistake. I told Elizabeth.

It just came out. The guys were on their second cheeseburgers when Elizabeth and I went to the rest room.

"You must have been really hungry," Elizabeth commented, washing her hands at the sink. "Your lipstick's all over your face."

I looked in the mirror for the first time since we'd left the gym and saw that my lipstick was almost up to my nose.

"Something really weird happened," I told her. "I poked my head in the broom closet to say that Mr. Ormand wanted us to cut out the finale, and whoever was in there pulled me inside and French-kissed me."

Elizabeth froze with her hands over the sink.

"You don't know who it was?"

"No. Brian was in there part of the time, but there were other guys I hardly knew. I mean, it was *dark* in there."

"Somebody you don't even know had his tongue in your mouth?" Elizabeth cried.

"Yes . . ."

"Alice, that's the next thing to being raped!"

"Well, not exactly."

"You were violated!"

The more she kept at it, the worse I began to feel.

Pamela came into the rest room then, and she was the last person I wanted to know, because she's going with Brian. What if it had been Brian who'd kissed me?

But Elizabeth just barreled on.

"Alice was violated," she said.

"What?"

"The next thing to being raped," said Elizabeth.

"*What?*" Pamela cried.

I had to tell her.

"Alice, that's exciting!" she said.

I looked at Elizabeth. Elizabeth looked at Pamela.

"Pamela!" Elizabeth said sternly. "Somebody she doesn't even know had his tongue in her mouth!"

"That's what I mean!" said Pamela. "A perfect stranger! The Mystery Kisser! Just think, Alice, you'll go all through eighth grade looking at every boy and wondering, 'Was it him?' 'Was it him?'"

Pamela should have gone to that bridal shower, not me.

By the time Mr. Price came to pick us up, I decided I had two lunatics for friends, and when Patrick and I got in the backseat beside Pamela and he put his arm around me, I wondered if he could sense that something was different.

As soon as I got in the house, Lester said, "Well, she's back from the dead—Dracula's daughter."

Dad was sitting at his music stand with his flute, trying out some new sheet music. "Have a good time?" he asked, leaning forward to turn a page.

"I was violated," I said.

All the expression went out of Dad's face, and Lester lowered the sports page. I'll admit, I enjoyed having *something* exciting to announce for a change.

"What happened, Al?" asked Dad.

I told them about the haunted house and the broom closet and how somebody had given me a French kiss. A couple of them.

Dad looked relieved when he found out it was only a kiss. "Where in the world were the teachers?" he asked.

"They were all over the place, but they couldn't be everywhere at once."

"I guess you're right," he said. "Well, I'm glad it wasn't anything more than a kiss." That really got me. Didn't he *care*?

"I was still violated!" I insisted, sounding more like Elizabeth by the minute. Something outrageous had happened to me, and nobody was paying attention.

"Well, you don't know who it was, so you might as well forget it," Les said. "Be more careful next time."

"Somebody was responsible for that!" I declared.

"So what do you want Mr. Ormand to do, Al? Apply thumbscrews till one of the eighth-grade boys confesses?" he asked.

"If it had been *you* in the closet . . ." I began.

"I keep out of closets," said Lester. "Besides, the poor guy probably did it out of self-defense. If someone cornered *me* in a closet wearing black net stockings and a peacock feather headdress and enough makeup to sink a ship, I probably would have grabbed the first thing I could put my hands on, too."

"That is so *typical!*" I shrieked. "It's always the girl's fault. If she's molested or raped, it's always because she asked for it."

Lester tossed his magazine over his shoulder and threw back his head. "Okay, okay! Have Mr. Ormand line up all the boys in eighth grade and shoot every fifth one till somebody comes clean. Will that satisfy you?"

I didn't know what I wanted. I wanted to be noticed, but not too much. I wanted to be kissed, but not too hard. I wanted to be like everyone else, but at the same time I wanted to be different. I wanted excitement and adventure, but I also wanted protection. Thirteen must be the year of the split personality, that's all I could figure out.

The phone rang just then, and I went out in the hallway to answer. It was Elizabeth.

"Alice, I just called Patrick and told him what happened," she said.

"You *didn't!*"

"I thought he should know. I mean, a boy has a right to know that the girl he kisses good night is damaged goods, so to speak."

"What?" Elizabeth was worse than Lester.

"And he said he already knew."

"What?" *Brian,* I told myself. It was Brian, and he was going around bragging to everybody.

"So who was it?" I asked.

"Patrick."

"*What?*" It seemed the only word I knew.

"Listen, I'm going to hang up because he's going to call you," Elizabeth said. "But everything's okay now, because it was only Patrick."

Were we all crazy or what?

I hung up after she did, and sat with my hand on the phone. About five seconds later, it rang.

"Yes?" I said, in about as cold a voice as I could manage.

"Alice?" said Patrick. "Listen, I don't know why I did that. Because it was just the two of us there in the closet, I guess."

"So if it had been just the two of us in the closet, would it have been okay to rape me?" I asked.

"Who's talking rape? I thought maybe you'd like it. I mean, you wouldn't know who it was, and it would be sort of a mystery. Besides, the way you were dressed . . ."

"Patrick, it was just a costume. I'd never been a showgirl before."

"Well, I'd never been a zombie before, so I didn't know how to act. Okay?"

After I hung up, I wished I *hadn't* known it was Patrick. I realized it *would* have been nice to wonder which of the other guys might have done it. What was I making such a fuss about?

I sat there looking at myself in the hall mirror—the peacock feather headdress, the makeup. This is what I needed, I decided. A whole new look. A whole new personality.

The phone rang still again.

"Alice?" came Pamela's voice. "I've just broken up with Brian."

"What?" I croaked again for about the fifth time.

"After I got in the car, I started thinking about that kiss in the broom closet, and realized Brian was back there most of the evening. So I called him up and accused him of French-kissing you behind my back."

"What did he say?"

"He didn't say much of anything. He just kept saying, 'What?' He certainly didn't deny it."

"So you . . ."

"So I told him he was a sneak and a cheat, and it was over between us. I'm a free woman. I might even go back to Mark."

5

A Touch of Green

Even after I told Pamela that it was Patrick, not Brian, she still said she was breaking up with Brian, that he was a dork. Handsome, all right, but a real dweeb.

I couldn't get it off my mind that weekend. Pamela had broken up with Mark in the first place to go with Brian, and now she was breaking up with Brian to possibly go back to Mark; Elizabeth had broken up twice with Tom Perona; when would it happen to Patrick and me? I mean, if he could grab me and French-kiss me without even telling me who he was, couldn't he just call sometime and say, "Hey, Alice, I'm going with somebody else now"?

Maybe I wanted this to happen. I like Patrick, *really* like him—better than any other guy I've ever known—but will I always feel this way? Sometimes he does really stupid things. What if I met someone I liked better?

What I was thinking of in particular was Crystal's wedding and the reception afterward. What did I know about receptions? The groom's younger brother, my escort, was seventeen. What if it turned out I liked—*really* liked— Peter's brother?

Dad was making waffles on Sunday morning, so both Lester and I migrated to the kitchen about the same time.

"What do you do at a wedding reception?" I asked. "I've got to know what to expect."

"Eat," said Lester, spearing one of the waffles and putting a big hunk of butter on it, where it melted into little square pools of yellow.

"At some point, someone will toast the bride and groom, and you'll raise your glass like everyone else," Dad told me. "A lot of time will be spent taking photos of the wedding party—that kind of thing."

"You'll dance," said Lester, reaching for the syrup.

I let my waffle drop off the end of my fork. "Dance?"

"Yeah. Dance. As in moving your feet," said Lester.

Something told me that at a wedding reception people didn't just face each other and jiggle their shoulders. They put their arms politely around each other, held hands, and moved in step, and I knew that however they danced at wedding receptions, I didn't know how to do it.

"I can't dance!" I wailed, my eyes suddenly brimming over. "Dad, I can't be in this wedding! I'll ruin everything!"

"Al, pipe down!" Dad said. "Why is it that everything is the end of the world for you? Crystal's wedding will go off whether you can dance or not."

"Teach me!" I begged. "Right now."

"It's four weeks off, Al. You still have time to eat your breakfast," Dad said.

As soon as we finished, though, I hung over the back of his chair until I knew he couldn't stand it anymore.

"Okay, let's get this over with," Dad said.

He went into the dining room, over to our stereo cabinet, and took out a dusty square box of small black disks.

"What *are* they?" I asked.

"Forty-fives," Dad said. "This was way back in the Olden Days, Al. In fact, these belonged to my uncle. I was the musician in the family, so he gave his collection to me."

He opened our ancient record player, which was about as dusty as the box, and put on one of the forty-fives.

"Okay," he said, "this is a waltz. They usually play at least one waltz at a wedding reception. You have to think *one,* two, three, *one,* two, three. . . . On the first beat, we take the longest step, and then two smaller steps to catch up."

ONE, two, three, ONE, two, three, I counted to myself, and suddenly Dad was guiding me backward. My feet were falling all over each other, but he gripped me fast and kept me moving. Then I got the hang of it, and we were really traveling. I was *dancing!*

Dad started to smile, and we took even bigger steps. Through the living room, back into the dining room again, around the table, out into the hall . . .

"I'm doing it, Les!" I called. "I'm waltzing!"

"Bully for you," said Lester. "Just don't fall in the punch."

"This was one of our favorite songs, Marie's and mine,"

Dad said. "'Fascination.'" And he began to sing while we danced: "It was fascin-a-tion, I know . . ."

I loved dancing with Dad and hearing him sing. I thought of him waltzing around with my mom, especially when he got to the last line, about fascination turning to love.

When the music ended, I said, "What if it's *not* a waltz? What if it's something else?"

"Well, kiddo, I guess you'll have to wing it. I'm pretty rusty in the dance department. I just sort of make it up as I go along."

"How do *you* slow-dance, Lester?" I asked when the record was finished.

"I just put my arms around Marilyn and we move side-ways from foot to foot," he said.

"Does Miss Summers dance?" I asked Dad.

"We've danced some," he said.

I couldn't believe I'd only asked one question but gotten the answers to two, so I took a chance: "How close do you dance?"

"Close enough to keep our feet going in the same direction," Dad said.

Lester was studying all weekend for a huge exam, so I called Elizabeth, but she and her family were taking the baby to visit relatives up in Pennsylvania, so I asked Pamela if I could come over.

"I need a new look," I told her when she met me at the door. I think maybe Pamela was feeling the same way, that we needed something to rev up our lives, something that would make people really notice us. "In fact, I need a whole new personality. A brain transplant."

"Never mind the brain, let's work on your face. You need a new eye shadow," Pamela said.

"A *new* eye shadow? I don't wear any."

"Then that's the problem. Your eyes don't stand out. How can you have any personality if you haven't got eyes?" She looked at me closely. "Green. If you wore green eye shadow and green eyeliner to match your eyes, it'd be perfect."

She got some cosmetics from a drawer, and I sat on the edge of her bed while she did my whole face.

"Blush," she said. "Eyeliner. Lip liner. Mascara . . ."

When I looked in the mirror, I hardly recognized myself. Like Pamela said, though, my eyes sure stood out.

"That's *you*, Alice! That's your color!" Pamela said excitedly. "See what it does for you?"

It was the first time anyone had suggested I had a color. Miss Summers had called me Alice Green Eyes once, but she hadn't said I had a color. I had a type! I *was* a type! There was a color that was distinctly me!

"Here. You can have these," Pamela said, giving me the green eye shadow and eyeliner. "They don't work for me. I'm blue."

I made a detour over to the drugstore on Georgia Avenue on my way home and bought some mascara.

Then I sauntered into the house and sprawled on a chair across from Lester, who had his books and papers all over the coffee table. I picked up the comics and pretended to read.

"Holy . . . ! What *is* it?" said Lester. "Halloween's over, kid."

"It's the real me, Lester! It's my color!" I said defiantly, lifting my head so he could get the whole effect.

"You look like something raised from the dead!" he insisted.

Dad came in from the kitchen and looked at me. "You're not really going to go anywhere looking like that, are you?" he asked.

I lost it then.

"You don't know anything about makeup and fashions, so why don't you both just shut up!" I snapped.

"Al, I guarantee that if your mother were here, she wouldn't let you out of the house looking like that," Dad said.

"Styles change! Fashions change! She'd at least keep up with what was going on, and color's big right now! Everybody has a color, and mine's green!" I yelled.

"But you look like you're decaying! You're beginning to mold!" Lester argued. "Al, you look sick around the gills! You look like a dead fish!"

I burst into tears and ran upstairs. Unfortunately, the tears made the eyeliner run, and my face was a mess, but I fixed it up the best I could. I would not give in.

I took a green sweater and held it to my chin in front of the mirror. The green around my eyes seemed to leap out. Green was me, all right.

"What did you do to your eyes?" Elizabeth asked the next morning at the bus stop.

"Pamela fixed them up for me. We discovered my color, Elizabeth. It's green!"

She studied me some more. "Well, it sure makes your eyes stand out," she said at last. She didn't exactly say she liked it, but I figured she had to have time to get used to it.

When Patrick got on the bus, though, carrying some posters for the fall band concert, he stopped right by my seat and stared. "What happened to your face? Your *skin* is green!" he said.

"It's the style, Patrick," I said, and for the second time in a week, he seemed just plain stupid to me. What kind of boy looks at a girl and asks, "What happened to your face?"

The fact was, I didn't much care whether he liked it or not. The reason people were staring was that they weren't used to me looking dramatic. They were so used to the "innocent Alice" look that they had to get used to the idea of Alice McKinley with a little pizazz.

But Patrick just wouldn't quit.

"Well, if you're going green, how about carrying this around for me?" he said. He held up one of the posters about the band concert, with the word CONCERT in big green block letters.

"Why not?" I said.

"Wait a minute. Better idea!" Patrick took the roll of tape he was going to use to put up the posters and taped two of them together, back to back. "Stand up," he said. I did, and he hung them over my shoulders like a sandwich board.

At first I felt angry at him, but when everyone on the bus started to laugh, I realized they were laughing with me, not at me.

"Okay," I said. "I'll wear this all day."

Patrick looked surprised. "You will?"

I shrugged. "You asked me to wear it, I'm wearing it." All the kids clapped.

At school, everyone looked at me, pointing and laughing, and I just laughed along with them. Miss Summers noticed, too. She was passing my locker and stopped to talk. Her eyes were the bluest I'd ever seen, even though she has brown hair, not blond. She had on a gray and blue and lavender dress that sort of changed colors when she walked.

"Well, you're looking different these days, Alice!" she said cheerfully. "In fact, you're a walking advertisement!" She laughed. "How are things going?"

"Great!" I said. "But I miss having you for English this year."

"I miss having you in my class, too," she said, and smiled at me with her beautiful blue eyes. I noticed that she didn't wear blue shadow, though. I wondered what color she wore.

The thing is, I *liked* being noticed—being a little bit crazy, a little bit wild. I loved going down the halls at school with Patrick's sandwich board around my neck, and I didn't want the day to end. There had to be something more I could try. I was ready. Boy, was I ready!

6

Shock Wave

That evening, before I went to the Camera Club the next day, I decided I'd better ask Lester if I could have the camera Crystal had returned after they broke up. I doubted Dad would want me to use his.

Lester and a bunch of his guy friends were in the living room watching Monday night football, and I knew better than to ask him a question during the game. I waited till the team was standing with their arms around each other, then edged over to Lester's chair. Les had one fist in a bag of Fritos and the other in the air, cheering the team on.

"Lester . . ." I whispered.

"Later!" he said. "I'm watching the game."

I pointed to the set. "They're just standing there talking," I protested.

"That's a huddle, kid," said one of his friends. "Okay! Here we go!"

The players lined up, but then they stood around some more, bent over with their hands on their knees. I don't understand football at all. A minute later all the players were piling onto everybody else, and Lester leaped to his feet.

"Touchdown!" he yelled. You couldn't prove it by me.

"Lester," I said again when a commercial came on.

"*What?*"

"Did you have any plans for that camera you gave Crystal? The one she returned. I've signed up for the Camera Club at school and I need it."

"Actually, I was going to wrap it up and give it to you for Christmas."

"Lester!"

"Merry Christmas, Al. It's yours," he said, and waved me away.

I took it to Dad, who put in a roll of film, showed me how to adjust it for distance, and how to work the flash.

"Have fun," he said, handing it back. "First roll of film's on me. After that, you pay for the film and developing. Okay?"

I realized then that it would have been a lot cheaper to sit around the Explorers' Club and talk about trips on Amtrak than it was going to be to take pictures. I was thinking about going back in the living room and asking Lester if— since this was to be my Christmas present—he'd throw in a couple rolls of film, too, but he and his friends were absolutely mesmerized by the game.

"I'll bet I could walk in there naked and they wouldn't notice," I told Dad.

"Well, don't try it," he said.

The more I thought about it, though, the more curious I got. One of the guys put his feet on the coffee table, all the magazines slid off, and he didn't even look down. In the movies, of course, a brother's friends always think his kid sister's cute, and she grows up and marries one of them. It could happen!

I went upstairs, took off all my clothes, and put on my bathing suit. Then I casually walked through the living room, picking up empty bottles and cans. The guys didn't even look in my direction. Everyone was yelling at the quarterback.

So I went back up and put on the peacock feather head-dress I'd worn on Halloween, and this time I paraded slowly around the living room. I guess I caught a commercial, be-cause suddenly Lester muted the sound. Without even looking, I knew that all eyes were fastened on me.

"What *is* it?" somebody said.

"Swat it, and see if it flies," said someone else.

"Al, go upstairs and get human," Lester told me.

Suddenly I rushed back up to my room, my face as red as ketchup. They didn't think I was cute, they thought I was demented. I caught one glimpse of myself in the mirror and ripped off the headdress.

Would I *ever* grow up? I wondered. This was the kind of thing I might have done back in fifth or sixth grade; I couldn't believe I'd tried something so ridiculous now.

"Nice try," Lester said later, and I did something even more stupid. I got up and slammed my door.

The next morning I set off for school, camera in my book bag, to make my second try at getting a life. At noon, how-ever, something happened I didn't expect. There's a new guy, Justin Collier, who's in my English class. He's not quite as good-looking as Mr. Everett, but he's tall and looks as though he'd be a lot of fun. He was passing our table in the cafeteria with two other boys and stopped to kid around with us. Elizabeth was really thrilled.

"Hey, Green Eyes, you're in my English class, aren't you?" Justin asked me.

"You're just now noticing her?" Pamela quipped. She had her eye on Justin, too.

"Hey, gimme a break! I'm a transfer student," Justin said. "My dad's in the navy."

"So we're supposed to salute?" Pamela asked. I mean, when Pamela's on the prowl, you know it.

"Whooaa!" said Justin. "Who's the babe with the blue eyes and the sassy mouth?"

"Pamela Jones," I said. "I'm Alice, and this is Elizabeth."

"Hi," Elizabeth said, and smiled.

"Hi, Pamela Alice Elizabeth," said one of the other boys, trying to balance his empty tray on Elizabeth's head. She giggled.

"Anyway, I was supposed to get a course outline and never did. I wondered if I could borrow yours and make a copy," Justin said.

"That's one of the oldest lines in the book! Alice, don't fall for that," said Pamela.

"Hey, Blue Eyes, what'd I ever do to you?" Justin said. "I *need* it! I'll take it to the library, make a copy, and bring it right back."

"Never trust a guy six feet tall," Pamela said, grinning.

"Ha! Never listen to a girl with blue on her eyes!" said Justin. "You girls always hang out together? The three hot mamas?"

We giggled some more.

"All but Elizabeth," Pamela joked. "She's going to be a nun."

I couldn't believe Pamela said that. It was as though she was jealous of Elizabeth, and was trying to put her down. First of all, it's not necessarily true. And second, even if it was true, it made being a nun sound like an insult. I could almost feel Elizabeth shrinking beside me.

"No kidding?" Justin Collier looked at Elizabeth. They were all looking at Elizabeth, and her face was so red, she looked as though she had a fever.

Pamela noticed, too, of course, and immediately tried to backpedal: "I mean, she'll probably be one of those nuns who's so hot, she's kicked out of the convent, but . . ."

"Pamela, shut up," I whispered.

Elizabeth was as angry as she was embarrassed.

"Don't mind her," she said to Justin. "She's naturally hot. Her parents are nudists."

I felt as though I were sitting between two erupting volcanoes. Pamela had never told us *not* to tell anyone about her parents, but somehow we just knew that the information was confidential.

Not anymore.

"Heeey!" said one of the boys, turning again to Pamela. "You go to those sunbather camps, huh?"

"Man, just tell me where you meet and give me a pair of binoculars," said the third guy. They were all leering at Pamela.

I thought she'd go along with it. I thought she'd enjoy all the attention and laugh it off. Instead, Pamela leaned forward and stared around me to give Elizabeth a long, withering look. Elizabeth glared right back.

I quickly snatched my English outline from my notebook and gave it to Justin. "You can keep it till tomorrow, but be sure to give it back," I said.

The guys loped off, leaving the three of us there at the table. I could feel knives passing through me, left to right and right to left.

Suddenly Pamela got up, pushed her chair in with a bang, picked up her tray, and left. Elizabeth got up, picked up her books, and went out by the other door. It was as though they were both mad at me! Was eighth grade nuts or what?

Patrick came by on his way to band, carrying a pair of drumsticks and rapping out a little rhythm as he went.

"What's this?" he asked, stopping by the table. "Eating alone?"

"I am now," I snapped.

"What's wrong? You mad or something?"

"Everything's wrong," I said. "I'm sick of eighth grade."

"Why? I think it's great!"

"You would," I retorted. "Any guy who would grab a girl and pull her into a broom closet and French-kiss her without even letting her know who he is would probably love this lunatic asylum."

"That was three days ago!" Patrick said. "You going to remember it forever?"

"Well, it was stupid."

"Okay, so it was dumb. I thought you'd enjoy it, that's all. You didn't, so sue me."

"You could at least apologize."

"I'm sorry you don't have a better sense of humor," Patrick said, and walked away.

I was near tears when the bell rang, but at least I had the Camera Club to look forward to after school. Unless, of course, we all had to sit in a circle and show each other our baby pictures or something.

The first surprise was that we met in the biology lab. The second was that the club's sponsor, Mrs. Pinotti, was a tiny little woman who looked for all the world like a sparrow. She wore wide canvas shoes, shaped almost like a duck's foot; she had a sharp nose like a bird's beak; a lined face; closely cropped brown hair, like feathers; black beady eyes; teeny little hands; and she was dressed in a brown turtleneck and slacks. She was also fascinating.

Because I'd missed the first couple meetings, I was spared

the sessions on the mechanics of a camera and listened to this tiny woman talk about how the great photographs are a whole lot more than pretty pictures.

"Anyone can see a pretty scene and snap it," she said. "The artistry comes in looking at your subject in a new way. Capturing its shadows, taking it from an unusual angle, photographing just a piece of it up close. The great photographs—the ones we remember—capture feeling, soul, mood, action, and drama. The rest end up on picture postcards."

A number of kids were nodding, but this was all new to me.

"In the next two weeks," she said, "I'd like you to shoot a whole roll of film on a single subject. It can be one person or one group—a family, a couple; it can be a room at different hours of the day, a garden—but I want all thirty-six exposures on the same subject. Let's see how much variety we can get on a single theme. I'll try, too."

After that I sort of sat on the sidelines and listened to the other kids talk about what they were doing with their cameras. I learned that the photo shop across the street would sell us film and develop it at half price when we showed our club membership cards, so I paid my three-dollar dues and became a member.

A guy named Sam wanted to try out his flash attachment and asked another girl and me to pose for him while he checked it out. I didn't know any of the kids well and felt

more of an explorer here than I had at the Explorers' Club.
Here I was investigating new territory without Pamela,
Elizabeth, or Patrick around. It was lonely and exciting
both.

Pamela came over around eight and her eyes were red. I
took one look at her and said, "Come on up."

We sat on the edge of my bed and she said, "I don't think
I can ever forgive Elizabeth for telling about my folks."

"I know," I said, "but you shouldn't have said what you
did, either. She's just as mad at you."

"What *I* said was supposed to be a compliment. I mean,
what girl wouldn't want guys to think she's so sexy that if
she ever joined a convent, they'd throw her out?"

"Elizabeth, that's who."

"Well, she should have stopped to think before she said
what she did about my parents," Pamela said, and reached
for a tissue.

"I just don't see what the big deal is!" I told her. "You told
us! How were we supposed to know you never wanted us
to mention it to a living soul? And besides, what's wrong
with your folks' being nudists? They don't think it's wrong,
so why should you?"

"Because I don't want anyone talking about my parents!"
Pamela said, and suddenly I was astonished to see her break
into tears. "Oh, Alice," she sobbed, leaning against me.
"They're separating."

This was just too much.

I put my arm around her. "Why? When?" I tried to remember when I'd seen her parents last. Hadn't they gone to a movie together sometime last summer? Didn't that mean anything?

Pamela just went on crying but finally straightened up. "I don't know why. Mom just told me tonight. I think someone else is involved, but I'm not sure."

"Your dad's moving out, then?"

"No. My mom."

Her *mother?* Mothers sometimes left their families? *Mothers* got involved with somebody else?

"What are you going to do, Pamela?" I asked softly.

"I'm staying with Dad. I'm not the one who wants to leave. Mom wants me to go with her, of course, but I'm not. Now they're fighting over that."

"Oh, Pamela!" My tissue box was empty, and I had gone to the hall closet for more when I heard the doorbell and went downstairs.

It was Elizabeth.

"I will never forgive Pamela Jones for what she did today," she said.

I pulled her inside. "Oh yes, you will. Her folks are separating."

Elizabeth's mouth fell open, and her eyes grew huge. "*Why?* Because of what I *said?*"

With Elizabeth, original sin begins with her.

"No. Her mom's taking off. She might be seeing someone else, Pamela thinks. Pamela's up in my room right now, crying."

Elizabeth ran upstairs ahead of me, and as soon as she got in the room, she had her arms around Pamela, and Pamela was saying, "I'm sorry," and Elizabeth was saying, "I'm sorry," and I was just standing there on my rug trying to think how I could keep from growing any older than I was right then. If life got any more complicated, I'd need an encyclopedia of instructions.

Lester passed my door, paused long enough to hear all the "sorrys" going on, and disappeared in a flash. I heard his door close, then lock, at the end of the hall.

I pulled out the pillows from under my spread, propped them against the headboard, and we lay in a row, our feet stuck out in front of us.

"I wish I could go back to last summer, before I knew about my folks, and just stay that way forever," Pamela said softly, her nose clogged.

"I wish I could go back to Mrs. Plotkin's class," I told them. "When I was in her room, it was as though she could handle anything that happened to us."

"I wish I could go back to before Nathan was born," said Elizabeth. "Life was so simple with just Mom and Dad and me."

But we couldn't go back and we knew it. Life was going forward whether we wanted it to or not.

I didn't know how I felt about Patrick, Pamela didn't know

how she felt about her mom, and Elizabeth didn't know how she felt about Justin Collier. Every time she'd seen him in the hall that afternoon, he had called her "hot mama" and she hated it.

There was a soft knock on my door.

"I'm making popcorn downstairs, if anyone's interested," called Dad.

And for a little while, the world seemed good again as we traipsed down to the kitchen and filled our bowls from the electric popper.

7

Outrageous

"Did your life change after I was born?" I asked Dad the following evening. We were both working at the dining-room table. I was doing homework on my side and he was writing checks on the other, and I wondered if he and Lester ever wished *they* could go back to a time when life was simpler.

"*My* life did!" Lester said from the living room. "The mess! The smell! The crying! The burps!"

I ignored him and concentrated on Dad.

"We were so ready for you, all the changes seemed like good ones," Dad said. "I don't know if I ever told you, Al, but your mom had three miscarriages before she finally had you."

"She *did?*"

"Each time she was so disappointed. And finally, you were the one who took."

I thought that over. "If any of the other eggs had hatched..."

"Not *hatched,* Al. If any of the other fertilized eggs had gone full term..."

"It would have been someone else, not me. Right?"

"Right!" chimed in Lester. "A boy! Twin boys! Anybody but you. Just my luck."

Pamela came over later. She said her mom was moving out that evening and she didn't want to be around. Her parents weren't speaking except to her, and she was tired of being a messenger service.

"'Tell your mom the stereo stays,' Dad says. 'Tell your dad to go to hell,' Mom answers. No, thank you. If they've got anything to say, they can say it to each other." -

"I'm really sorry, Pamela," I said. "Why don't you stay all night?"

"I will," she said, and sheepishly admitted she had already stuffed her pajamas in her school bag.

Up in my room, I told Pamela how, if Mom hadn't lost her other three babies, I'd probably be someone else, only Pamela said it wouldn't have been me at all. I just wouldn't *be*. And then we started thinking about all the eggs that never get fertilized and all the sperm that never make it to the egg, and how, purely by accident, there were hundreds and trillions of people who never got to be born at all. Somehow, that made Pamela feel better, I think. I mean, being born and having your parents separate was still better than not being born at all.

"What I'd like," said Pamela wistfully, "is to be anyone but Pamela Jones for the next month. The next *week*, even. To just float right out of all that's going on at home and not be myself again till it's over."

"I wish you could," I told her. Then, "Me? I'd like a new personality. More than green eye shadow. I mean, I'd like to develop a whole *look*, you know? Not so . . . well . . . virginal!"

"So let's dye your hair green," said Pamela.

"Are you kidding? I'm going to be in a wedding party the end of the month."

"Just the smear-on kind of dye. You can wash it right out. It's mousse, actually. We'll both go to school tomorrow with our hair dyed green and sticking straight up on one side of our heads, slicked down on the other."

I looked at Pamela. She looked at me.

"Let's do it!" I said.

We walked to the drugstore and bought the stuff.

We had to set the alarm for an hour earlier the next morning so we could get out of the bathroom before Dad and Lester wanted in. We dressed, me in a green turtleneck, Pamela in a purple one. Then we took some old towels into my room, closed the door, and took turns applying the thick green gel to each other's hair. The hair that stuck straight up in spikes made our scalps look like the back of a stegosaurus.

"We've got to do the eyebrows, too," said Pamela, so we did each other's brows.

By the time I put on my green eye shadow and liner, I looked like a New Age leprechaun. Pamela dressed the same, except she wore blue eye shadow.

"Ready?" I asked, and we went downstairs together.

Les had already left for the U, but Dad was putting things in his briefcase when he looked up and saw us. I watched his lips part in slow motion.

"Al, what's this?"

"We're just trying out a new look," I said. "Relax. It washes out."

"You're not going to school that way?"

"Yes! It's just a look, Dad. I wanted to try something new."

Pamela moved on ahead of me into the kitchen and grinned helplessly from beyond the doorway.

"I don't think so," said Dad. "Go upstairs and wash it out."

"Dad . . . !"

"Al, I'm interviewing a clarinet instructor at eight o'clock and I'm late. I don't have time to be standing here arguing. Do as I say."

I stood frozen to the floor. He was embarrassing me in front of Pamela.

He put on his raincoat, picked up his briefcase, and stared at me hard. "I mean it," he said, and went on out to the car.

"Gee, I thought he had a sense of humor!" Pamela said. "What are you going to do?"

"There isn't anything *to* do," I insisted. "There isn't time! I'd miss my bus, and we haven't had breakfast." I went out in the kitchen and got some English muffins, split them in half, and dropped them in the toaster. "I'll tell him it was either missing school or going like I was."

We ate quickly, then threw on our jackets, and went down to the school bus stop. We turned heads, all right.

"Oh, my gosh!" Elizabeth squealed when she saw us.

At first I was afraid she'd be mad we hadn't included her, but when I explained about Pamela's mom moving out and Pamela needing a distraction, she just shrugged.

"Mother wouldn't have let me, anyway," she said.

Everyone on the bus was laughing and feeling our spikes, and we each wore a big dangly gold earring on the spike side of our heads.

Patrick, however, didn't like it. He got on the bus, stared at me for five seconds or so, and then, without a word, moved to the back of the bus and started talking to the guys about football. What was it with boys, anyway? Were they afraid to be a little different? Try something new?

But everywhere we went, kids turned and laughed and pointed at us. The seventh graders positively gawked. One of them even came up and asked where she could buy the green mousse. Sometimes when I walked into a classroom, the kids clapped, like I was famous or something. I guess that must be what it feels like at the Academy Awards, going to the ceremony in your wildest clothes with everyone looking at you and taking your picture. Someone even took our picture for the yearbook. The only thing wrong was that the people I cared most about weren't all that excited about it. The people I hardly knew thought we were great.

Most of the teachers just gave me a "Well, it's weird, but it's your hair" kind of look, and let it go, but most disappointing of all was Miss Summers's reaction. I passed her coming out of the library and she said, "Oh, Alice!" and gave me a sort of desperate look.

Well, I was getting one thing straight, I decided as I walked to the cafeteria. I was getting across the fact that I wasn't sweet little Alice McKinley anymore—a generic type of girl with no imagination or style. The kind of girl you gave teddy bear earrings to and expected her to wear them.

Justin Collier hung out at our table at noon and tried to stick pieces of gum wrappers and stuff on our spikes. I noticed that although he was kidding around with Pamela and me, it was Elizabeth he was flirting with.

We did look weird, I'll admit it. I ducked in the rest room before fourth period and saw that one of my tall green spikes had fallen over, and my mascara was smeared.

Pamela and I were still laughing when we gathered up our books at two-thirty and went out to the bus. The wind was blowing hard, and all Pamela's spikes were leaning to the left. Elizabeth tried to straighten them up, and we laughed some more. Then I heard Pamela say, "Uh-oh."

I looked around and saw Lester's car parked there in the

No Parking zone, just ahead of the buses. He got out and walked toward us.

"Over here, babe," he said, taking me by one arm. The other kids stared.

"*Les*-ter!" I said, trying to pull my arm away, but he had it in a viselike grip.

"Oh, boy! Big brother's mad!" I heard one of the guys whisper.

"Yeah, he's cute when he's mad," Pamela said, trying to make a joke of it, but Lester wasn't smiling.

I knew if I really fought Lester, I'd make a scene, so I pretended it was all a joke and rolled my eyes, laughing, as I managed a final wave. He ushered me into the passenger side of his car, closed the door, and came around to the other side. Without a word, he started the engine and drove off, just as a second bus beeped at him.

"Since when did I get a private chauffeur?" I asked.

"Since you proved you couldn't be trusted," said Les, and he sounded different. Serious.

I glanced over at him. "Dad called you, right?"

"Right."

"At the U? He had you paged out of class just for this?"

"I only have morning classes today. He called me at home."

"And told you to wait for me after school and see whether or not I'd washed the stuff out of my hair?"

"Brilliant deduction."

"So what's the big *deal?* I didn't shave my head, did I? I didn't pierce my nose or do anything permanent!"

"You disobeyed Dad, and that's enough."

"And you never did, I suppose?"

"Of course. I just didn't have a brother to come get me."

I banged my books down on the coffee table when we got inside and clomped up to my room, slamming my door so hard that the walls rattled. I think I even heard a small chunk of plaster tumble down inside the walls.

How *could* Dad do that to me? In front of all my friends, have Lester cart me off as though I were three years old? And why would Lester agree to do it? I heard once that people who were wildest as kids often turn out to be the strictest parents. Lester must be getting in some practice. I whirled around, clutching my dresser top to vow an oath of revenge, then gawked at the sight in the mirror before me. Four of the five green spikes had fallen over, some to the left, one to the right, so that my head looked like a pineapple. I must have been resting my head in my hands a lot that day, because the green gel had slid down one whole side of my face. The eye shadow had moved on over to my cheeks, and with the dark smudge of mascara, I looked like a raccoon.

Well, so what! I thought angrily. It was just a joke. Just for fun. I didn't say I was going to go all week like that, did I?

I went in the bathroom and took a shower, washing my

hair and face, and had to use Ponds cold cream to get all the mascara off. By the time Dad came home, I was doing my algebra at the dining-room table. I didn't say anything and neither did he. It was like we were living in a monastery and had taken a vow of silence.

I was hoping that when we sat down to dinner, Dad and Lester would keep the conversation going and I could show how mad I was by not joining in, but even Lester had vowed eternal silence. He reached for the peas and onions, helped himself, then put the dish back down again. Nothing.

At first I decided I could hold out as long as they could. I could go the rest of my life not talking, if that's the way Dad wanted it. I could graduate, move away and marry, and I still wouldn't open my mouth. But by the time Dad put some carrot cake on the table, my favorite, I said, "You had no right to send Lester to school to pick me up."

"Oh?" said Dad. "I thought I was the parent here."

"Parent, not dictator! Since when can't I fix my hair the way I want? You never said anything about it before."

"You never looked like something out of *Night of the Living Dead* before," Lester put in.

"So I wanted a new look! I just wanted to try it. It was only for a day." I turned to Dad. "You really overreacted, you know? If you send Lester to drag me home just because I mousse my hair, what are you going to do if I smoke a cigarette? Cut my hand off? If I have sex with a guy, will you

68

burn me at the stake?" I was shaking, I was so angry. "You have no idea how you embarrassed me in front of my friends by having Lester come for me at school."

"Then perhaps you have no idea how you embarrassed *me* by going to school looking as you did," Dad replied.

"*How?* You weren't even there!"

"Someone I happen to care about is in that school, and it embarrasses me to think she might have seen you, that's why."

He had actually said the words "care about." He cared very much about what Miss Summers thought. I wished I could tell him she *hadn't* seen me, but he'd find out from her, I knew.

I put down my fork. "Okay, get it over with. Punish me. Ground me. How long is detention? What's the new curfew?"

"No punishment," said Dad. He took a bite of cake, then a sip of coffee. But he wasn't smiling. "I just want you to know that I am very disappointed in you."

I think that was the first time I could remember that Dad said that to me. It was worse than any curfew. The carrot cake in front of me looked like a chunk of cement that I couldn't possibly swallow. I stared at it a moment longer, then put down my fork and left the table.

I didn't know this could hurt so much. It would have been better if he'd slapped me, but what right did he have to be disappointed just because I looked weird for a single day?

69

Then I thought about those knee-length shorts he wears sometimes in the summer. They're supposed to be madras, only they're this disgusting red, yellow, and green plaid. Sometimes when he gets home from work, he doesn't even bother to change his dress socks and shoes. Just takes off his trousers and puts on those shorts, and he looks *awful*. So maybe I did understand how Dad felt about me going to school with green spikes on my head.

I stayed in my room most of the evening. Both Pamela and Elizabeth called to find out what was happening, and I pulled the extension phone into my room.

"What *happened*, Alice?" Pamela asked. "That was so *dramatic*, Lester's coming to carry you off."

Dramatic?

"Nothing's happening," I said. "Dad's just disappointed in me."

"But it was only an experiment! You want me to come over and apologize to Lester for talking you into it? I'd *love* to apologize to Lester. I'll do anything he wants."

Pamela's had a crush on Lester ever since I can remember.

"No, thanks," I said. "I'll have to get out of this myself."

Elizabeth had a different reaction. After I told her that Dad wouldn't punish me, that he was just disappointed, and how awful that made me feel, she said, "See, Alice? That's why it helps to be Catholic. You go to a priest to say your confession and do your penance, and then you feel all free and forgiven."

I went downstairs where Dad was sewing a button on his shirt cuff.

"I'm thinking about becoming a Catholic," I said.

"Oh? What started that?"

I sat down across from him. "Since you said you're disappointed in me. Elizabeth says all I'd have to do for forgiveness is confess to a priest and do penance. With you, there's no end. It's purgatory forever."

I wasn't sure, but I think Dad was trying not to smile. "Well, I don't think you have to convert or anything."

"What, then? Shave my head? Crawl to school and back on my hands and knees?"

"How about just telling me the next time you want to do something drastic. I don't mean every little thing, but we are talking *weird* here, and I think you know it."

"Then how about promising me never to send the gestapo after me?"

"You promise not to be weird, the gestapo won't be necessary."

"As though *he* never disappointed you! What about the time we went to the ocean and Lester had Marilyn in while we were gone?"

"I was disappointed in him, then, of course, but tonight we're talking about you."

I sat watching Dad sew on his button and realized that

maybe when you love someone, it isn't always the same. You could be disappointed in him one day and go right back to loving him the next. Maybe you could even be disappointed in him and go on loving him, both at the same time.

"You know what's weird?" I said. "Love's weird."

"One of the weirdest things there is," said Dad. "No explaining it at all."

8

Studies in Forgiveness

Pamela began spending more and more time at our house, and before the Camera Club met again, I took a lot of photos of her. I told her it was our assignment, that I had to get used to my camera.

At first she wanted to make sure her hair was combed and her makeup perfect, but after a while she didn't seem to care. She more or less ignored me. I caught her sitting on my bed with her legs drawn up, chin on her knees. I took the way she looked in the morning after a shower, her hair wet and clinging to her head above the collar of her robe, no makeup. I caught her reading a magazine. Stretching. And because I was looking at Pamela with different eyes, I saw a lot of things I hadn't seen before.

When I picked up my prints, though, I realized how amateurish they were. Some of them were all washed out—my exposure was wrong. Or Pamela was facing away from the light and her face was in shadow. At least half the pictures looked too posed, too false, or the composition was all wrong—a vase seemed to be growing out of the top of her head—stuff like that.

But out of the thirty-six prints, two of them held my attention—the one of Pamela with her chin on her knees, and one of her looking out the window. The first had the saddest expression I had ever seen on her face. Her eyes looked wet, and her mouth tugged down at the corners. In the other photo she appeared angry.

Somehow I felt that although I didn't want to make a career of photography, I would be happiest in a job where I studied people. In learning more about Pamela's feelings, I was learning more about myself.

"Soul!" Mrs. Pinotti said at Camera Club, holding up the print of Pamela looking out the window, and the others agreed.

"Everyone's so polite," I said to Sam. He's dark-haired and sort of chunky. "Nobody asks what was going on with Pamela when I took that shot."

"That's because Mrs. Pinotti says she believes the same as primitive people—that when you take someone's photo, you take a piece of their soul. So we don't ask any more than the photographer wants to tell us."

I liked this club, I decided. I liked Mrs. Pinotti; I liked Sam. And I liked what I was learning about the kind of work I might like to do someday.

We all compared prints with each other, and one thing we discovered was how many pictures you have to take to get even one that's outstanding. As I was making my way toward the door at the end of the meeting, Sam called, "Hey,

Alice, thanks for posing for me last time so I could try out my flash. Want the print?"

"Sure," I said.

I couldn't believe what I saw—two girls side by side, but one of them, with strawberry-blond hair, had two huge greenish eye sockets. It looked as though a child had taken a bright green crayon and drawn circles around both my eyes. That *couldn't* be me! I couldn't look that awful! I stuffed the photo in my pocket, then slipped into the rest room as soon as I was out in the hall.

For a long time I stared at myself in the mirror. And when I got home, I threw out all the green eye shadow and liner. At school the next day, no one seemed to miss them.

"Hey, you look really nice today," Patrick told me.

"Thanks," I said.

Justin Collier began hanging around Elizabeth at school. Like I said, he wasn't as good-looking as Mr. Everett, but he was cool enough. He was tall, and that got him a lot of attention from the girls. He had his eye on Elizabeth, though. Pamela had gone overboard to attract his attention, and it was Elizabeth he fell for.

He was in our biology class, too, and always seemed to be looking in Elizabeth's direction. He smiled at her every chance he got. When he came to class, he'd detour by the window just so he could stop at Elizabeth's desk and talk, and when class was over, he'd wait outside the door and walk with her to wherever she was going.

"Gosh, Elizabeth, aren't you *thrilled?*" Pamela asked her. "I know a dozen girls who'd love to trade places with you, me included."

Elizabeth would just turn pink and say how he was too tall for her or too forward or too silly or something, and the more casually she treated him, the more he hung around. She was pleased, though. We could tell.

Elizabeth's the Young Advocate for her church's missionary fund, whatever that is; I went over to her house one day after school and helped address envelopes to all the young people in her church, asking them to pledge something each month to the missionary fund. But just when we'd think she only cared about serious stuff, she'd do something different with her hair, or go to the mall with us to meet Justin—by accident, of course. Then she'd walk around with him, looking gorgeous. There are times she's not as nutty as I think. Times I start to believe that with all her hang-ups, she's going to be at the starting gate long before Pamela and I show up.

At home, I concentrated on getting back on good terms with my dad. I had the table set each night when he came home, whether it was my night to cook or not; I made sure I kept my stuff picked up and not strewn all over the living room, and when I got back from school on Thursday and realized that every pair of jeans I owned was dirty, I put them all in the washing machine and added the clothes in the hamper, just to save Dad and Lester some work.

Mistake. Lester had a new red sweatshirt in the wash, and when I opened the lid of the machine, everything that was white before was now pink, including Dad's undershirts, shorts, some pillowcases, and a white linen shirt of Lester's.

I stared down at the clothes. How could this happen? How could I continue to do one stupid thing after another? I went straight to the phone and called Aunt Sally in Chicago.

"Oh, my goodness!" she said when I explained the problem. "I can't believe I let you get to eighth grade without teaching you how to sort the wash."

No matter what happens, see, Aunt Sally figures it's her fault. I could lose my life skydiving, and Aunt Sally would say it was her fault for not giving me lessons.

"Listen, dear," she told me, "here's a little poem that helps. My grandmother taught it to me, and if you recite it every wash day, you'll know exactly what to do:

> If it's white, and red it's not,
> Make the water doubly hot.
> If the clothes are bright and bold,
> Keep the water rather cold.
> Never mix your white and blue
> If you'd keep your colors true.
> If your whites are stained, then reach
> For a jug of chlorine bleach."

The silence over the line was awesome.

"But what do I do now?" I whimpered finally. "I've already ruined a whole batch."

Aunt Sally explained how I should fill the washer again with cold water, a little detergent, and a cup of Clorox, put all the white stuff back in, and soak them for an hour.

"Whatever you do, Alice, don't put them in the dryer," she said. "Keep changing the water and soaking them in bleach until all the pink comes out. Once you put a stain in the dryer, it's set for life."

I didn't think I could stand it. There were unpardonable sins all over the place! Everywhere I looked there were mistakes that could not be undone. And this, of course, happened to be the night that Lester wanted to wear his white linen shirt. But after I soaked all the pinks in chlorine bleach, the only one that stayed pink was Lester's shirt.

"Has anyone seen my white linen shirt?" he asked. "Marilyn and I are going to a concert, and we wanted to stop by a club afterward."

I took a deep breath. "Lester," I said, "there was an accident."

"An accident," he repeated, staring at me. "Someone broke their arm and you used my shirt for a sling?"

"Well, worse than that. Unless, of course, you want a *pink* shirt. Now if you want a *pink* shirt, then it looks great!"

78

"Someone was bleeding to death and you used my shirt for a tourniquet?" he croaked.

"A washing machine accident, I mean," I said miserably. "I was t-trying to be helpful. I *thought* I was doing you a favor."

Lester followed me down to the basement and stared at the pink linen shirt hanging there on the line. "I'll take care of my own clothes from now on, okay?" he said angrily. "That was a thirty-eight-dollar shirt, Al!"

"It's still perfectly good! It's just pink!"

"If I'd wanted a pink shirt, I would have bought one. Jeez, Al! Use your head! Who would wash a red sweatshirt and a white linen shirt in the same water?"

Worse yet, when I folded the clothes later, so much red had come out of the sweatshirt that even *it* looked more pink than red. Not only that, but because I had put it in the dryer, it was two sizes too small.

Patrick came over on Friday and asked if I wanted to go to a movie. When we got there, though, the show was sold-out, so we just hung around the mall. We went into a tie shop and Patrick tried on the loudest, wildest tie they had. They don't like that in tie stores, especially if you're thirteen, but then, they never know who might buy something.

We ended up at the Orange Bowl for an orange freeze, and Patrick said that Mark Stedmeister was interested in going with Pamela again, now that she'd broken up with Brian.

"She's got a lot on her mind these days," I told him.

"Yeah, Mark told me about her folks."

"What she probably needs more than anything else is just friends to listen when she wants to talk."

"Mark can listen," Patrick said.

"Mark's a dweeb."

"How come?"

I looked at Patrick and wondered if boys ever remembered anything. I'll bet that all the embarrassing things that happen to them just drift right out of their heads afterward. With girls, these memories stick around forever. They *implant!*

"Patrick, don't you remember what Mark did to Pamela the summer between sixth and seventh grade?" I asked.

Patrick stopped drinking his orange freeze and looked at me blankly.

"When she was showing Elizabeth and me a new bra she had bought, and Mark came up behind us and grabbed it out of her hands and went racing around the playground, waving it like a flag?"

"That was a *year* ago!" Patrick said. "*More* than a year, and she's gone out with him since!"

"It doesn't matter if it was a hundred years ago, or that she went with him again. It happened, and girls *remember!* Mark's a *dweeb!*"

"She's going to hate him forever because of what he did after sixth grade?"

"Well, what about what he did last summer? When he pulled open the back of her bathing suit and dumped his potato salad in her pants?"

"Yeah, I guess that was pretty stupid."

"See, Patrick? *You'd* never do anything that dumb," I said confidently. "Except for that stupid kiss in the closet, you would *never* do anything like that."

Patrick didn't answer, just kept sucking on his orange freeze.

I grinned at him and leaned across the table so he had to look at me. "What's the stupidest thing *you* ever did to a girl?"

No answer. Patrick kept sucking away like a vacuum cleaner.

"Well?" I said, teasing.

"You don't want to know," he said.

"I asked, didn't I?"

"You'll get mad."

"Why would I get mad?"

Patrick had reached the bottom of his drink. He lifted the straw out of his glass, turned the straw over, and sucked at the other end.

"Well," he said finally, "you remember last May—when we were all over at Mark's?"

"In May? They don't open their pool till June first."

"I know, but it was a warm day and we were playing badminton on the lawn."

"Wasn't I sick that weekend? Getting over the flu or something? I remember sitting around feeling woozy and watching the rest of you play. We made lemonade. Somebody brought over this big bag of lemons, and you guys were seeing who could suck a lemon the longest without making a face. Is that the day you mean?"

"Yeah, that's the day. Well . . ." Patrick whirled his glass around and around on the table between his fingers. "*Promise* you won't get mad?"

I began to feel uneasy. "I said I wouldn't."

"Well, the girls went inside once, all except you. You stretched out on the picnic table and fell asleep for a few minutes."

I vaguely remembered lying down on the picnic table, my sweatshirt folded up under my head, and I guess I did drift off. It was a warm day, and I was really out of it.

I looked over at Patrick. His face was turning pink.

"What happened?" I asked suspiciously.

"Well . . . I was just horsing around, see . . . you were asleep, and . . . it was just a joke, Alice, honest!"

"*Patrick . . . ?*"

"I took two lemon halves and set them on your breasts."

I blinked. I tried to imagine myself the center of attention on Mark's picnic table, *snoring,* even, with two lemon halves turned upside down, like cones, on my breasts, and all the guys laughing.

"Patrick!" I said again.

"I only left them on for a couple of seconds."

"Why didn't anyone *tell* me?"

"You think the guys would *tell* you? The girls never saw."

I shoved my drink away. "Patrick, when I got home that day I couldn't figure out why there were these stains on my T-shirt. I thought something was the *matter* with me, like I was *lactating* or something."

"See? I told you you'd be mad."

"But it was so stupid!"

"Well, you wanted stupid."

I was infuriated. "All this time you never told me."

"You never asked."

"How could I ask? I was asleep."

"That's just it. I couldn't tell you, because you were asleep."

Was this a dumb argument, or what?

"If you were asleep, Alice, you couldn't be embarrassed. And if you're embarrassed now, it's useless, because everyone's forgotten it already."

"Girls don't forget things. We remember them forever. They become a *part* of us, Patrick. They stick to us like Velcro." I picked up my shoulder bag. "I'm ready to go."

"See? You're mad."

"I'm disappointed in you," I said gravely, just like my dad.

"Well, I won't do it again. It was dumb, and I'm sorry."

I didn't feel like letting him off that easy, though. I guess

I wanted him to shave his head, crawl to school and back on his hands and knees, *and* promise he'd never do it again. But then I remembered how close I'd felt to Dad after he'd forgiven me.

"Okay," I said to Patrick. "Apology accepted."

9

Religion and Sex

On Saturday, Crystal Harkins came over to take me to her aunt's for my fitting. I'd told Marilyn at the Melody Inn that morning that I was going to be in Crystal's wedding, and she'd said, "Have fun!" I never saw a woman so happy about another woman's wedding plans. As soon as Crystal was out of the picture, Marilyn would have Lester all to herself.

It felt really strange to be in this grown-up world of weddings and fittings and measurements and stuff.

"Ready?" she asked, when I answered the door. "You're going to love your dress, Alice. It looks great! Danny was asking about you."

"Who's Danny?" I wanted to know, climbing in the car beside her.

"The guy you'll be paired with in the procession. Peter's brother."

"What's he like?"

"Well, next to Peter, of course, he's probably the handsomest guy in the world. Just kidding. But he's a real hunk."

I gave a nervous giggle. Whenever I'm nervous, I giggle. I imagined walking down the aisle on my own wedding day, giggling. It would be just like me.

"Are *you* nervous?" I asked her. "About the wedding and everything?"

She laughed.

"I'm nervous about the wedding, all right, but what's 'everything'?"

"Oh, you know. What comes after."

"The wedding night? Sex?" She laughed again. "No. Not really."

I was quiet and stared out my side window.

"Anything on your mind, Alice?" Crystal asked, and I remembered that this was the woman who had rescued me once when I had a permanent I couldn't stand, who showed me what to do with my hair. If I was ever to ask someone about sex, why not Crystal?

I took a deep breath. "What if after your wedding night, you . . ." I shrugged. "Well, what if you don't like it?"

"Sex?"

"Yeah."

"Why wouldn't you like it? It's a natural function."

"So is throwing up," I said.

"Listen, you like to eat, don't you? You like to sleep? To stretch? To sneeze?"

"But I don't like to eat *every*thing."

"Well, you don't have to *do* everything, either. You can tell your husband what you like and what you don't, and then you can try something else. What you've got to remember, Alice, is that sex isn't like what you see in the movies."

"*What* movies?" I asked curiously.

"Well, almost any movie. There are lots of ways to make love. Not everybody uses the missionary position, you know."

I was about to ask how religion got into it when Crystal gasped, "Oops! We just went through a red light, Alice. See, you've even got *me* flustered!"

Ten minutes later I was standing on a low stool in a gorgeous jade green gown while a woman holding pins in her mouth moved around me on her knees, hemming up my dress. She took tucks here and there, at my waist, at the bosom, until I looked as though I had been poured into that dress.

"Now!" Crystal's aunt said, rocking back on her heels. "Just don't gain any weight until the wedding's over, okay?" Then she turned to Crystal. "She almost looks like a Barbie doll, doesn't she?"

"That anorexic thing?" said Crystal. "No way. Alice, don't you ever get as bony and malnourished as that nitwit."

As she drove me home again, I said, "Crystal, could I ask you something?"

"About wedding nights?" She grinned.

"No. I just wondered if you ever . . . well, think about my brother anymore. Do you ever miss him?"

"I don't miss his going for weeks at a time without calling. I don't miss calling him only to find out he's with Marilyn. I don't miss being in his arms and thinking he really loves me, and then discovering he says the same things to Marilyn Rawley. No, I don't miss that at all."

"But don't you miss some of the good things?"

Crystal suddenly grew quiet. "Yes. Some of the good things I miss very much. But I love Peter now, and I simply don't allow myself to think of Lester," she said.

That worried me some. I would have felt better if she'd said she'd never loved anyone as madly as her husband-to-be.

I guess I was thinking about it at dinner that night, because I realized I'd tried to wind up a forkful of spaghetti five times, and finally Dad said, "Something on your mind, Al?"

I didn't want to tell Lester what Crystal had said in the car for fear it would really mix things up, so I tried to remember what else we had talked about. Wedding nights . . . throwing up . . .

"I thought missionaries were preachers," I said finally.

"Huh?" said Lester.

"This is a topic of conversation, Lester," I said primly. "I just want to know what they do."

"They don't usually preach as much as they go to foreign countries and teach people how to do things a little better," said Dad.

"Sort of like sex therapists?" I asked.

"What?" said Lester.

"They show people the right positions and everything?" Dad and Lester stared at me.

"Are we talking religion here, or are we talking sex?" asked Dad.

"Crystal said that there are lots of ways to make love," I said knowingly.

Lester dropped his fork. "When did you see Crystal?"

"We went for my fitting today, and we were discussing sexual intercourse, for your information."

Lester coughed.

"And *she* said that not everybody chooses the missionary position. So I was just wondering about missionaries."

Dad laughed. "Oh, honey, Marie would have enjoyed you so much at this age. It's too bad you only have Les and me to help you muddle through."

I still didn't understand. "So what's the missionary position, anyway?"

"Well, it's been said that when missionaries went to foreign countries in the past to convert the natives, they talked them into wearing clothes and giving up what they felt were unusual sexual practices. They taught them that the only acceptable way to have intercourse was with the woman on the bottom and the man on top. So ever since then, that's been referred to as 'the missionary position.' Got it?"

"What are the others?"

Lester looked at Dad. "Will she never quit?"

"I want to *know!*" I insisted. "How will I ever learn if I don't ask?"

"Okay," said Lester. "Woman on roof, man on ladder; woman in boat, man on water skis; man on table, woman on chandelier . . ."

"Cut it out, Les," said Dad. "Al, whatever position a man and woman find themselves in, they can usually figure out a way to make love, and whatever is comfortable and gives them pleasure is the right way. Okay?"

"Just for the record," Lester said, "what did Crystal say was *her* favorite way of making love?"

"Lester!" I said. "I'm surprised at you. I'm her bridesmaid, after all. You don't think I'd give away Crystal's secrets, do you?"

And I grandly got to my feet, went upstairs, and called Elizabeth.

"Elizabeth, you know that missionary fund you collect for?"

"Yes?" she said.

"Do you know what missionaries *do?*"

"What do you mean?"

"They teach natives how to have sex."

"*What?*"

I love to tell Elizabeth things about the church that she doesn't even know herself. "I just found out. They go to primitive cultures and show them the right position."

Elizabeth gasped. "How do you *know?*"

"Dad just told me."

"Alice, I've been collecting for the missionary fund for two years!"

"Well, think of all the good your dimes are doing," I said.

I was so thrilled with my new discovery that I had to tell Pamela, too. "Have you ever heard of the missionary position?" I asked. And then I forgot all about it, because I could tell that Pamela was crying.

"What's wrong?"

"I miss Mom and I don't want to leave Dad," she said, weeping. "Oh Alice, I've never been so sad in my whole life."

10

Emergency

l invited Pamela over to spend the night. I asked Elizabeth to come, too. Elizabeth's usually able to think of something comforting to say. I just didn't know what to tell Pamela. That, being motherless myself, I knew she'd get over it? Huh-uh. You don't get over it. Not ever.

We all lay on our backs on my bed and stared up at this big wispy spiderweb that blew back and forth in the draft from my heat register. Here we were in eighth grade, the last year of junior high, and Elizabeth was too insecure to go out with Justin alone, Pamela was too unhappy to enjoy herself, and I was soon going to be in a wedding where the bride might possibly still be in love with my brother. God, who made the world, sure must have a sense of humor, I decided.

"Where do you suppose we'll be ten years from now?" Elizabeth asked. "We'll all be twenty-three."

Twenty-three! It sounded so grown-up and far away. Older than Crystal, even.

"I'm thinking about being a psychiatrist," I said. It was

the first time I'd said that aloud. Actually, I'd been thinking about being a school counselor, but after seeing all the misery Pamela had been going through lately, I thought maybe I should go for the heavy-duty jobs.

"A *shrink?*" asked Pamela.

"Psychiatrist, psychologist, whatever," I said. "I just want to know why people do the things they do. Maybe stop some of the problems before they start. I think I'd like that."

"You just want people to tell you about their sex problems," said Pamela.

"They come to me with *sex* problems?" I said, wondering. I was a missionary, too, then?

"Pamela will know all about sex. She'll probably be married with two kids," said Elizabeth. "Three, even."

"What about you?" Pamela asked her.

"Maybe I'll join the Peace Corps. Maybe I'll travel. Be a flight attendant or something," said Elizabeth.

That was a new kind of talk from Elizabeth.

"I'm wondering if it's smart to get married," said Pamela. "You think everything's fine, and then—pow! I had no idea my folks were thinking about a divorce. One day we're all eating breakfast together, and the next day we're not."

"You can bet they talked plenty about it when you weren't around," I told her.

"Then it would have been better to talk while I was there so I would know it was coming. Figure out the whys. Why do you suppose people get divorced?"

"They meet someone they think they love more, maybe," said Elizabeth. "But maybe, after they divorce, they find out they don't."

"Maybe they grow apart; they're each interested in different things," I suggested. "Or maybe they just get tired of the missionary position."

"The what?" asked Elizabeth.

"Never mind," I said.

We had doughnuts and Cokes around midnight and went to sleep, but I woke up about four to hear Pamela crying. It's really strange to be in your bed and hear one of your best friends crying. My first thought was to get up and go over to the cot against the wall, but then I wondered if this was a private time for her.

I decided to turn over, just noisily enough to let her know I was semiconscious, but not loud enough to wake Elizabeth. I also gave a little sigh so she'd know it was me.

The room was quiet for a moment.

"Alice?" she whispered at last.

"Yeah?"

I heard her swallow, like the words were all choked up in her throat. I slipped out of bed and went over to sit on the rug beside the cot. "What's the matter, Pamela?"

"Oh, Alice!" She put out one arm and draped it over my shoulder, and I reached up and put one hand around the back of her neck. Her skin felt hot, as though she'd been crying a long time. "Th-this is the worst thing that's ever happened to me."

"I know," I said, and stroked her neck.

"I don't even know whether I love or hate my mom."

"You probably feel both ways," I said.

She sat up finally and fished for a tissue on top of my dresser.

"Subtimbs," she said, sniffing, "I really wonder if I can stand this. I mean it."

"Pamela," I said. "Do you remember back in sixth grade when we were in that play together, and I was jealous of you because you got the lead part, and I pulled your hair onstage?"

"Yes," she said, and blew her nose.

"I was horrible to you, and you were embarrassed, but you got over it and you were the star of the show. Remember when Mark grabbed your AH-H Bra and waved it around the playground? And Brian put gum in your hair and you had to cut it off, and you said it was the worst thing that had ever happened to you?"

"But it *wasn't!*" Pamela wept. "*This* is."

"I know, but you survived it. Remember when you lost your bikini top in the ocean? Maybe those were just rehearsals, Pamela, for real life, to prove that you can take it."

She kept on crying.

"You've still got a mom and dad," I said helplessly. "They just don't live together anymore."

"But I *want* them to," she wailed, and I couldn't think of any answer to that. A lot of good I was doing.

"Alice," she said finally, "I guess when I think about how things are with *you*, I should feel lucky."

"Yeah?"

"I mean, gee, you haven't had a mother since kindergarten, and your dad's going to let Miss Summers get away, and you'll be motherless all through high school and college. You won't even have a mom around when you get married!" She reached forward and hugged me. "Thanks, Alice. You've made me feel so much better."

"You're welcome," I said.

"Sleep tight," said Pamela.

I crawled back in bed beside Elizabeth and didn't get to sleep for a couple of hours.

Dad usually makes waffles for us when I have a sleep-over, but he was outside cleaning leaves out of our rain gutters, and Lester was gone for the weekend. He and Marilyn were visiting friends in Virginia and wouldn't be home till that night.

Elizabeth had to leave for Mass, and Pamela had promised to spend the day with her mother, helping fix up her mom's apartment, so they both left about nine-thirty. We'd had French toast, and I'd made extra for Dad and set it on a plate in the microwave so he could heat it up when he came in.

I did my homework, listening to his footsteps now and then on the roof, or the clunk of the ladder against the side of the house. And then I heard a scraping sound from the backyard, a yelp from Dad, a thud, and a horrible clatter.

I leaped up and ran outside. Dad was lying motionless on the ground, the ladder on top of him.

"Dad!" I screamed, and rushed down the steps. I pulled the ladder off and crouched down beside him, my mouth dry and my heart thumping so hard, it hurt.

Then I started crying. "Dad!" I said again.

His eyelids fluttered.

"Dad, please sit up," I said, and then I realized he might have broken his neck. "No, *don't* sit up!" I begged.

He sat up anyway. He kept blinking and shaking his head, and then he reached up with one hand and rubbed the back of his neck.

"Dad, are you okay? Is anything broken?" I asked.

He just kept looking at me and blinking, and finally he said, "It's not broken." He was staring at the ladder.

I'd never seen him this way and didn't know how to reach Lester. Finally I went inside and called Aunt Sally. No answer. It was Sunday, and she and Uncle Milt usually go to church and then out to eat.

I wondered whether I should call Mrs. Price, but when I looked out the window, their car was gone. Janice Sherman? No. I didn't want her over here scurrying around and giving orders as though she lived here. I picked up the phone book, looked up a number, and dialed Miss Summers.

The phone rang about five times, and I figured she was at church, too. Then she answered. She sounded breathless, and maybe a little irritated. "Hello?"

Oh, my gosh! I thought. What if Mr. Sorringer was there and they'd been making love?

"Hello?" she said again.

"Miss Summers? It's Alice."

"Why, Alice! What a surprise! I was outside raking and *thought* I heard the phone."

I was relieved. "I'm really sorry to bother you, but Lester's out of town and I don't know where to find him and I couldn't reach my aunt in Chicago. . . ."

"What's wrong?"

"Dad fell off a ladder."

"Where *is* he?"

"Here at home. He's sitting out in the yard, and I don't know whether to call an ambulance or not."

"Did he break anything?" she asked, and her voice was shaky.

"I'm not really sure."

When she came, she was wearing old jeans and a sort of ratty-looking sweater. It was about the worst I'd ever seen her look, and she still looked beautiful. She had a leaf stuck in her hair.

She hurried around the house with me and knelt down on the grass beside Dad, taking both his hands in hers.

"Ben? Ben?" she said, and shook his hands a little.

Dad started to stand up, then sat down again. "Sylvia?" he said in surprise, and I saw his fingers close around her hand. At least he knew who she was.

Miss Summers turned to me. "Who's your doctor?"

I was so frightened that for a moment I couldn't remember. "Dr. Beverly," I said finally.

Miss Summers went inside and looked up his number. Luckily, Dr. Beverly was on call. He asked Miss Summers some questions, then said that if Dad was moving around, we should get him in the car, and he'd meet us in the emergency room at Suburban Hospital.

We both went back out to Dad. He was standing up and still staring at the ladder. He looked as if he was just waking up.

"Ben, you've had a fall, and Dr. Beverly wants to see you," Miss Summers said. "Come on out to my car."

"But it's not broken!" Dad protested, trying to pick the ladder up.

"We don't care about the ladder, Dad, we care about you," I said. "Come on, now."

We got him in the backseat, and I climbed in front. Miss Summers took off like a race car driver.

It wasn't until we got to the hospital that it hit me. I stayed in the car with Dad while Miss Summers went inside, and it was the sight of the nurses and orderlies hurrying toward us, rolling a stretcher, that made me start to cry.

I thought of being in Holy Cross Hospital after Mrs. Plotkin had her heart attack, and thought about how Mom had died in a hospital back in Chicago. When Miss Summers poked her head in the window to tell me I could come inside, I was sobbing.

"Alice," she said. She opened the door and sat on the edge of the seat. She put her arm around me, and I rested my head against her sweater, which smelled delicious, and I cried like a kindergarten kid. I didn't care, I was so scared.

"Wh-what if he dies?" I gulped. "I couldn't stand it if I lost Dad, too!"

"Honey, I think he's got a little concussion, but I don't think he's in danger of dying," Miss Summers said. She stroked my hair, and even though my crying had stopped, I wished it hadn't, because I wanted her hands in my hair forever. She had actually called me "honey."

"Come on. They'll need us in there," she said, so I wiped my face and followed her inside.

I hate hospitals. I hate the smells and the sight of people who look as though they're dead already being wheeled rapidly along the corridors, and I hate the look of strange machines and the sound of weird noises. The only thing that made this bearable was that Miss Summers was with me.

We both talked to Dr. Beverly.

"I've checked him over, and his blood pressure and pulse are stable," he said. "But he's complaining of neck pain, so we've sent him to X Ray. I'll talk to you again in a little while."

"We'll wait right here," Miss Summers said, and we sat down on the row of plastic chairs along one wall. Miss Summers put her arm around me again. *Why* couldn't I ask her now if she loved him? Why couldn't I ask if she'd be sad if he died? This would be the perfect time for her to throw her arms around Dad and say, "Ben, please don't die! I need you!" Isn't that what he needed, the will to live?

"Do you remember your mother, Alice?" Miss Summers asked me.

"Not very well. I confuse her with Aunt Sally, who took care of us for a while. It drives Dad crazy."

Miss Summers smiled.

"Mostly, I guess, I remember her through the things she left behind. Some letters to Dad . . . her recipe file . . . her sewing box . . . some books . . . her pictures . . ."

"Those are all important," Miss Summers said, and patted my shoulder again.

I wondered if I'd made it sound as though I didn't need a mother, as though the things Mom left behind were enough, and I was doing just fine.

"I miss having a mother, though," I said in a whisper.

This time Miss Summers didn't say anything, just kept patting my shoulder and absently curling a lock of my hair around her finger. I wondered if I'd remembered to wash my hair that morning. After Elizabeth and Pamela left, *did* I wash my hair? Or was it all greasy and stringy?

It was almost forty-five minutes later that Dr. Beverly came back to the waiting room. He sat down in the chair next to Miss Summers.

"Well," he said, "the X rays are negative, but he's still a little woozy. I don't think there's anything to worry about, but I'd like to keep him here for observation for a couple of hours. If we don't see anything abnormal, he could go home this afternoon. Someone will have to check him every two hours for the first twenty-four, however."

"We will," Miss Summers said.

I was so relieved, I started crying again. I thought when I got to eighth grade all this would stop. I was a leaky faucet. Dr. Beverly just smiled at me and handed me a tissue from the table. After he left, Miss Summers grabbed my hand. "Well! *That's* good news! Why don't we go get some lunch!"

We walked out to her car, and I suddenly felt very self-conscious. "I look awful," I said. "I don't think I washed my hair this morning, and my eyes are all red."

"You just look like a girl who's worried about her dad, Alice, but if it bothers you, why don't we have lunch at my place? I've got some chicken salad, and I might even make us some hot fudge sundaes."

That perked me up in a hurry.

As we drove along, Miss Summers told me about the gigantic oak tree in her yard, and how much raking she has to do each fall, but she doesn't mind because she loves autumn. Suddenly I was *very* hungry. Starving, in fact. And then we were inside her house with her baskets of colored yarn and her slippers just inside her bedroom, and, through the door, her unmade bed. Almost the same as I remembered it.

"I love your house," I said, taking off my jacket.

"So do I. It's just the coziest place!" she said.

Miss Summers slipped off her ratty sweater. She had a T-shirt on underneath, and she either wasn't wearing a bra or it was a loose one, because her breasts sagged a little, but they were still pretty and soft-looking. I couldn't help wondering if Dad had ever touched her breasts.

"I don't know what I'd do if I ever lost my dad," I said.

"You would *cope,* Alice, you would cope," she said firmly. "Every single one of us has losses in this life, but I don't think you're in any danger of losing your dad anytime soon. Now. Do you want your chicken salad on lettuce or in a sandwich?"

We sat at her little breakfast table overlooking her backyard and the oak tree. I knew there was no way in the world I could ask the question I really wanted to know: whether she and Dad would marry, but I got as close to it as I could.

"I see you have Dad's picture!" I said delightedly when I noticed his photo in the next room on her end table. It was a photo I hadn't seen before, so she must have taken it. He wore a soft sweater and was leaning against a tree, arms folded, feet crossed at the ankles. He was smiling. It was a wonderful smile.

"Yes. Isn't that a good picture of Ben?" she said, glancing over her shoulder at the photo. "One of the best I have of him, I think."

That meant she had even more!

She changed the subject then to school, and we talked about the eighth-grade dance next spring and how, before I knew it, I'd be in high school.

But will you be my mother? I wanted to ask. It reminded me of a picture book somebody read to me when I was small about a baby bird that hatches while its mother's away. It falls out of the nest and asks each animal it meets, "Are you my mother?"

"I love being here," I said finally. Desperately. I wondered if I was carrying it too far.

Miss Summers looked at me quietly for a moment with her gentle blue eyes and then said, "And I love having you here, Alice. But if your dad is going to be discharged this afternoon, he's going to want you there with him. What do you say we call the hospital and see what Dr. Beverly can tell us?"

I finished my sandwich while Miss Summers went in the other room and dialed the hospital. Then I took my dishes to the sink to rinse them, and as I passed the refrigerator I saw a batch of photos stuck there with magnets, and one of them was of Mr. Sorringer, our vice-principal, standing with his arm around Miss Summers on the deck of a sailboat.

I wanted to tear it off the refrigerator. He had a boat? He took her sailing? He put his arm around her and they went sailing off into the sunset?

But then I realized that Dad's picture in the other room

was in a far more prominent place and it was four times as big, so that had to count for something.

It was her bedroom that would tell the most, I figured. Whichever man's picture was in her bedroom was the one she most wanted to see before she went to sleep at night, the man she most wanted to dream of. I couldn't leave her house without peeking into her bedroom.

"Well, your dad's ready to come home, Alice," Miss Summers said, coming back into the kitchen. "I even talked with him. He says that from now on, Lester can clean the gutters."

"Great!" I said. "Could I use your bathroom before we go?"

"Certainly," she said, and I headed for her bedroom.

"There's one right there in the hall, Alice," she called.

I stood in the doorway of her bedroom, wanting terribly to go in, but she was watching. Reluctantly I turned and went to the bathroom in the hall. We left without my ever knowing whose photo she kept by her bed.

11

Rehearsal

"Well, I guess I put on quite a circus," Dad said when we walked in the emergency room later. He was sitting by the door with an attendant.

"I was scared, Dad," I told him. "Lester wasn't home, and I didn't know who else to call."

"I hope you're not apologizing for calling *me!*" Miss Summers said. She bent over and kissed Dad on the forehead. "How are you feeling, Ben?" One hand lightly massaged his arm.

"Giddy, but not quite so out of it as I was."

"Well, they wouldn't be sending you home if they didn't think we could take good care of you."

"Sylvia, I hate to be such a bother."

She leaned closer as though they were having a private conversation, but I heard her say, "Now that's a word that isn't even in our vocabulary."

"Our." She said "our," as though they had a secret language or something! I beamed.

The attendant insisted on helping Dad out to the car and

strapping him in the front seat beside Miss Summers. I crawled in back, happy to see them sitting together.

As we drove home, Miss Summers said that she was going back to her house and make some soup after she let us off, and that if I would check on Dad while she was gone, she'd take over after dinner and stay until Lester got there.

Dad seemed normal enough as he went up the steps between us, and after we got him seated on the couch with the Sunday paper, Miss Summers went on home. Dad leaned back and closed his eyes, and I flew around straightening up the house so if Miss Summers decided to stay awhile, she wouldn't think we lived like pigs. Every so often I'd go over to Dad, though, and pull open one of his eyelids with my thumb and finger to see if his pupils were dilated.

"Okay," he said finally, "I can see I'm not going to get any nap today," and he picked up the newspaper.

Elizabeth called.

"Alice, what happened? We saw you and Miss Summers helping your dad up the steps a while ago."

I told her about Dad's falling off the ladder, and how Miss Summers was coming back with our dinner. She obviously called Pamela, because that's who phoned next. "Is Miss Summers going to stay all night?" she asked.

"Why would she stay all night?"

"He's sick! They're in love! She wants to be close to him! He needs her!" Pamela said. Dad falls off a ladder, and all Pamela can think about is sex.

The next time I checked Dad, he was sound asleep and snoring, the newspaper on the floor, so I decided to let him be. When he woke up about forty minutes later, he said he felt a hundred percent better.

"Good! Miss Summers is coming over after a while with our dinner."

"Then I'm going to shower," said Dad.

I went up and sat down outside the bathroom door to make sure he didn't fall or anything, and a few minutes later I heard him singing in the shower. I wasn't sure, but I think it was "Fascination." I had to leave him once, though, when the phone rang. It was Janice Sherman wanting to tell Dad about a gorgeous piece of organ music she'd heard in church that morning, and how we ought to buy it for the store. I could hear an orchestra playing in the background. I guess I always wondered how Janice Sherman spent her weekends. I imagined her sitting at a desk writing letters to her cousins and listening to Vivaldi. I don't know Vivaldi from Verdi, but I know they're the kinds of composers she'd listen to.

I told her about Dad's falling off the ladder.

"Oh, my goodness! How is he?"

"Well, we had him in the emergency room, but he's better now," I said. I was careful not to say who "we" were. Janice has been in love with my dad since he became manager at the Melody Inn.

"Poor Ben!" she said. "If there's *any*thing I can do . . ."

"I'll tell him," I said.

O—O—O—O

The minute I hung up, Dr. Beverly called to ask how Dad was doing, and I said he was singing in the shower.

"That's a good sign," he told me.

It was after eight when Miss Summers came back. Dad had just finished watching *60 Minutes,* and Miss Summers walked in carrying a cardboard box with six plastic containers of her soup, two loaves of bread, some oranges, and a bouquet of mums from her garden.

"How's the patient?" she asked me, taking her stuff to the kitchen. Then she saw Dad sitting at the table with a ginger ale. Even I could smell his aftershave. "Ben McKinley, what are you doing all shaved and dressed?" she asked.

"Waiting for a lovely nurse to bring my dinner," he said.

It was good soup, with lots of onions in it, and the bread was thick and warm, with little pieces of herbs. I was chattering on about hospitals and how much I hate them when we heard Lester come in.

He hung up his jacket in the closet and sauntered on out to the kitchen, then came to a stop.

"Hello? Did I forget we were having company, Dad?" he asked.

"Hi, Lester," said Miss Summers, smiling. "Of course you didn't. It's a surprise visit, that's all."

"This whole day has been a surprise," said Dad, and he filled Lester in on what had happened.

"So I get here after all the heavy lifting, huh? Hey, Dad,

next time you try this, at least wear Rollerblades so they can wheel you around," Lester joked.

It was fun having Lester at the table. He made Miss Summers laugh, but he could also be serious. At one point he and Dad and Miss Summers were all discussing Tolstoy's novels, and I could tell by the way Dad sat back, listening to Lester argue his case, that he was enjoying the conversation.

See what an interesting family we could be? I implored Miss Summers with my eyes, but she was already bringing out another surprise: homemade rice pudding with cinnamon on top. "Not exactly the most exciting dish in the world, but it goes down easily," she told Dad.

The doorbell rang, and I went to answer.

There stood Janice Sherman, holding a large aluminum pot with a cover on it. It must have still been hot because she was wearing oven mitts. Before I could say a single word, she walked right in.

"This is absolutely scalding, Alice, but I thought the best thing I could do for Ben would be to make him a pot of my potato-leek soup. I'm famous for it, you know," she said as she headed down the hall toward the kitchen. "I hope I'm not too late for . . ."

She never finished her sentence. I saw her pause in the doorway, and heard the clunk as she set the pot on our stove.

"We love potato soup!" I croaked, following her in. "Janice, this is . . . I mean was . . . my English teacher, Sylvia

Summers. Miss Summers, this is Janice Sherman, Dad's assistant at the Melody Inn."

Miss Summers had popped a bite of bread in her mouth and swallowed hastily. "I'm so glad to know you," she said.

"I didn't realize you were already eating or I could have brought it later," Janice said stiffly.

"Janice, you didn't need to go to all this work, but it was very thoughtful of you," Dad told her. "Won't you sit down and have some supper with us?"

Was Dad crazy? I wondered, but I guess he knew she'd refuse.

"Oh, no. Actually, I'm rushing home to watch *Masterpiece Theatre,*" Janice said, taking off the oven mitts and thrusting one in each pocket of her coat, where they stuck out like ears.

"Are you a fan of that program, too?" asked Miss Summers. "You could eat some soup and watch it here."

That *did* bother me. If a woman was in love with a man, why would she want another woman staying for dinner? To test the competition?

But Janice wasn't about to take the consolation prize. "Actually, I've got my own dinner in the oven," she said, which I'll bet was a lie, because I know if Dad were alone and had asked her to stay, she would have let her food burn in order to keep him company. "But thanks, anyway. And Ben" —she put one hand on his shoulder as though he belonged to her— "take care of yourself."

"I will, Janice. With all you nurses around, I can't do anything but get better."

"Do you really think she has dinner in the oven?" I whispered to Lester after Janice left, and Dad and Miss Summers were putting food away.

"As likely as an ingrown toenail on the end of her nose," he said, and we laughed.

We told Dad and Miss Summers to go relax in the living room while we cleaned up.

"Thanks, Les, I hoped you'd say that," Dad told him.

"I've got to be going soon," said Miss Summers. "I still have papers to grade before tomorrow."

"You can at least stay long enough to enjoy the fire I built the other night, then forgot to light," Lester said. "Marilyn called, and I just never got around to it." He took some matches off the shelf and went into the living room. I heard him rolling up newspaper as Dad and Miss Summers followed him in.

When Lester came back to the kitchen, he said to me, "Well, I've done my part. The rest is up to Cupid."

"Do you think she loves him, Les?"

"He loves her, that's obvious."

"But . . . ?"

"If she doesn't, she's certainly put a lot of time into looking after someone she doesn't care about."

"She cares, but does she *love* him?"

Lester sighed. "Define love," he said cynically, and then, "I get any mail today?"

"Today's Sunday."

"Oh. Right." We rinsed the dishes off and set them in the dishwasher, and then he said, "Dad told me he got an invitation to Crystal's wedding. I just wondered if she mailed one to me and it got lost or something."

"I didn't see any."

"Then I suppose not." He put detergent in the dishwasher and closed the door. "I guess I thought we could at least be friends."

"Wouldn't it be a little embarrassing to have you there, Lester? Maybe it would bring back memories she'd rather not have on her wedding day."

I was putting the best spin on it I could, and Lester perked up. "That's probably it. Yeah, I suppose that's it. What's Dad giving her, do you know?"

"A gift certificate for the Melody Inn. Help them start a really nice CD collection."

"Yeah, she'd like that," said Lester.

We stayed in the kitchen as long as we could, not wanting to bother Dad and Miss Summers. I wanted her to realize how easily she could have lost him, if not to illness, then to Janice Sherman. I wanted her to know how lonely she'd be if she had, and how she belonged here, on our sofa in front of the fireplace. The fact was, of course, that Dad *hadn't* been about to die, she *hadn't* almost lost him to Janice Sherman, but didn't she have any imagination?

Later, when I passed the doorway to put Janice's pot in the refrigerator, I saw Dad and Miss Summers by the front door.

She had her coat on and they were standing about three inches apart. He had his hands on her waist, and she had hers folded behind his neck. They were smiling at each other.

I moved quickly away, but I couldn't resist one last peek. This time she was in his arms with her hands on his chest, his chin resting on top of her head. They were rocking slowly from side to side, as though dancing to some music only they could hear—the most gentle, loving embrace I'd ever seen.

I swallowed and wiped my eyes with two fingers.

"What's the matter?" asked Les, hanging up the towel.

"Love," I said, and sniffled.

On Monday, of course, Elizabeth and Pamela wanted all the details, and we were still talking about it when Mr. Everett was starting class.

"It's fate," said Elizabeth with certainty. "I think God planned it so that your dad would fall off the ladder on a day that Miss Summers would be home, so that they would end up in each other's arms."

"I don't know," I whispered back. "Couldn't God have thought up something a little less dangerous?"

"If it was less dangerous, Miss Summers wouldn't have been so concerned, and she might have just visited him at the hospital, and that would be that," said Elizabeth.

"Miss Price," said Mr. Everett, "why is it that whenever I'm ready to start the class, you are not?"

That wasn't exactly true. Most of the time, Elizabeth was

more than ready. I guess even the best teachers are entitled to an off day now and then, but Elizabeth embarrasses easily, and her face turned as red as her notebook. This was the second time he'd singled her out. She sat with her eyes on her desk for half the period, and when the bell rang at last, and I apologized to her, telling her I was as much at fault as she was, she said, "Well, one good thing, anyway; I'm not in love with Mr. Everett anymore."

The following Wednesday, I dressed in my best shiny black pants, a white rayon blouse, and a red-and-gold vest that my cousin Carol had sent me for Christmas. Crystal had said someone would pick me up at six for the rehearsal and the rehearsal dinner, so I watched out the window, my coat over my arm.

"It *does* seem a strange time for a wedding," Dad said, walking through the rooms, emptying the wastebaskets. The rehearsal was the night before Thanksgiving, and the wedding was to be the day after, which meant everyone would pig out on the day in between—Thanksgiving. "The bride might eat so much, she won't fit into her gown."

"What are *we* doing for Thanksgiving?" I asked. Sometimes Dad makes a reservation at a restaurant and we all go out.

"Lester's invited Marilyn, and I've asked Janice to join us," Dad said. "Sylvia's going to fly to her sister's over the holidays. They haven't seen each other in a long time."

"Oh," I said. Ever since Janice Sherman had her uterus

removed, I think Dad's felt a little sorry for her, and includes her when he can. But I don't think a woman should go around using her hysterectomy to get special attention, and I still wished it was Miss Summers instead of Janice.

The phone rang. It was Patrick.

"Hi. What'cha doing?"

"I'm dressed like you wouldn't believe. The rehearsal dinner," I told him. "Crystal's getting married on Friday."

"Oh, that," said Patrick. "Wouldn't it be weird if the minister forgot and pronounced them man and wife during the rehearsal, and they figured since they were already married they could just skip the wedding, so they went on their honeymoon two days early, and when people came to the wedding the bride and groom were gone?"

Had Patrick always been like that, I wondered, and I just hadn't noticed?

"Yeah, that would be a scream," I said as the doorbell rang. "Hold on a minute."

I put the phone down and opened the front door. There was this handsome guy, and I knew right away it must be the groom's younger brother.

"Alice, I presume?" he said.

I smiled. "Yes. Danny?"

"At your service," he said. "Everybody was rushing around like mad back at the hotel, so Crystal asked if I'd pick you up."

"I'm ready," I said. Then I remembered Patrick. "Just a minute." I picked up the phone again.

"Who's that?" asked Patrick.

"Danny, brother of the groom. He's driving me to the rehearsal. I've gotta go, Patrick."

"Well, go! You've got a bathroom, haven't you?" Patrick said, and laughed.

"I mean it."

"What's this guy look like? Tall, dark, and handsome?"

"Now that you mention it, yes. Listen, I really . . ."

"How old is he?"

"Patrick, I'll talk to you later, okay?"

"What time will you be back?"

"I don't know. Late. See you!" I said, and hung up.

"Boyfriend?" asked Danny as he helped me on with my coat.

"Something like that," I said, and felt guilty. Patrick might act immature sometimes, but he was still one of the nicest guys I knew. Not that I'd known all that many, of course.

Dad walked in from the dining room.

"Oh, Dad, this is Danny . . . uh . . ."

"Carey," said the boy. "That's French. Just kidding."

Dad smiled wryly. "You the driver?"

"Yes, sir! Want to see my license?" Danny made as though to take out his wallet.

"That won't be necessary. I'll take your word for it if you promise to get my daughter there and back safely. You won't be drinking, I trust?"

I was embarrassed that Dad was treating me like his precious little daughter and, at the same time, pleased that I *was* precious to him.

"No, sir! Your designated driver," Danny said, turning to me.

We went out to his car, and Danny opened the door for me, then went around and got in on the driver's side. "Better fasten your seat belt," he said. "Your dad's watching from the window."

I laughed.

He asked what kind of music I liked, and I said, "Any kind," so he turned on the radio and got some jazz. The church wasn't very far away, maybe twenty minutes from our house, so we didn't have to make conversation for long. He said he was a senior in high school in New Jersey and had applied to seven different colleges. He wanted to go into engineering.

"Are you thinking about a career yet, or is eighth grade a little soon?" he asked.

"Oh, no, it's not too early to think about that," I said. "I've given it a lot of thought, actually. I'm planning to become a psychiatrist."

"Really!" he said, and glanced over at me to see if I was joking. "Well! Interesting choice! Interesting people make interesting choices, so you must be fascinating."

"Very," I said, and we laughed.

Crystal's mother was orchestrating the rehearsal, and she wanted everything to go perfectly, so it made me a little nervous when I realized I'd be the first bridesmaid down the aisle. I kept reminding myself what Patrick had said, about the bride and groom getting married accidentally during the rehearsal and taking off, just to keep my sense of humor.

As I was standing at the altar, though, in the V shape Mrs. Harkins had arranged us in, I could see both Crystal and Peter and the pews for the congregation, and it seemed as though we were rehearsing not just for Crystal's wedding but for life: going through our paces, thinking about the "for better or worse." Nobody knew what would happen tomorrow even, much less ten years from now. Life suddenly seemed more serious than it had before.

But the rehearsal dinner was fun. Everyone piled into cars again and headed for a restaurant. By the time we'd all helped ourselves at the buffet table, I'd met about a dozen different people.

"*Where* did you say you'd met Crystal?" Danny's mother asked me as we both took a chocolate-covered strawberry at the same time.

"Just an old family friend," I said, hoping she wouldn't ask more. I popped another strawberry in my mouth, and I guess she figured I was in no condition to answer more questions, because she started talking to someone else.

Mr. Carey drove me home afterward. I guess I was a little disappointed. I was hoping I could see more of Danny. Dad was relieved simply to see *me*.

"I'm glad you're home safe, honey," he said. "I'll have to admit I'm not looking forward to the time your friends have driver's licenses and you're out riding around."

I kissed him on the cheek. "You've got two and a half years before that happens," I said, and went upstairs to change. I was thinking how Danny had perked up when I said I was going to be a psychiatrist. Like here was a girl who knew where she was going. Here was a girl with smarts. I wondered what he'd think if he knew I'd gone to school a few weeks ago with my hair in green spikes.

I guess that the kind of person you really are will win out in the end; it's not something, like green mousse, you can just apply. Everyone will know it's phony. Like Danny said, interesting people do interesting things, and I guess the way not to be boring was not to be bored myself.

I stood in front of my mirror to admire myself one more time before I took off my fancy clothes. I thought about Mom's three miscarriages and how very much she and Dad had wanted me. Who was this girl I was looking at? I wondered. A future wife? A mother? A psychiatrist? All three?

12

The Waltz

It was a strange Thanksgiving. For me, anyway. I suppose that for everyone else it was a great Thanksgiving. But for me the "big day" would arrive the day after.

Janice Sherman came bringing everything, practically, but the turkey and pies. It looked as though she had cleaned out her refrigerator. Marilyn brought the pies and rolls.

Sitting across from Marilyn and looking around the table, I wondered what everyone was thinking. Dad, I knew, was missing Miss Summers, but he'd rather she was with her sister than with Mr. Sorringer, that's for sure.

Janice was delighted to find that Miss Summers was out of town, and must have felt she had a chance with Dad, because she wore a wool dress that clung to her body like a wet T-shirt. Marilyn and Lester and I were probably the only ones at the table who were thinking about Crystal.

Marilyn was gay and sparkly, and took second helpings of everything. She looked as though she were ready to conquer the world—Lester, anyway—now that the competition was out of the way.

Les was quiet. He was serious and polite and acted about ten years older. Where would we all be and what would we be doing the *following* Thanksgiving? I wondered.

Marilyn left early because both she and Lester had papers to write over the weekend, and Les had a big exam coming up. But Janice hung around till every last piece of food was put away, the turkey carcass was picked over and plunked in the trash bag, and the dishes done. Once you let Janice Sherman in your house, she doesn't stop till the place is organized, and I was afraid she'd tackle our closets next. Dad tried to get her to sit down in the living room for a while.

"Are you sure there's nothing more I can do?" she asked.

"Only sit and watch this old man fall asleep," he joked. "Alice and I have a big day tomorrow, and I hate to admit it, but I'm tired."

"Well, it was a wonderful Thanksgiving, Ben. I loved being a part of your family," she said.

That was a proposal if I ever heard one, but Dad just gave her a squeeze, helped her on with her coat, and carried her dishes and containers out to the car.

"She's not, is she?" I asked him as soon as he came back inside.

"Who's not what?"

"A part of our family?"

"Not unless we adopt her or something."

"Dad, please don't marry Janice Sherman."

"Good grief, it never entered my head."

"Then let's keep it that way," I said.

As I passed Lester's room later, I saw him sitting at his desk with tablets and textbooks all around him. He stopped to stretch, tipping his head way back, and saw me standing in the doorway.

"What's this? A spy?"

I walked on in and leaned against his closet door.

"Could I ask a personal question?" I said.

"If I can answer it in thirty seconds." He took a drink of Pepsi from the can on his desk.

"Are you real upset you didn't get an invitation to Crystal's wedding?"

For once, he didn't try to turn one of my questions into a joke.

"In a way," he said. "I guess I'll have to look at Crystal as a lovely chapter in my life, and that's all. I've got the memories, and I really hope she and Peter are happy. He seems nice enough, from what I've heard."

"Good," I said. "And you're not the least bit sorry she made the choice for you, and that it's Marilyn you've ended up with, not Crystal?" Maybe I *would* make a great psychiatrist.

"Hello? Did I miss something here? Is Marilyn the last woman on earth?"

"No . . . I just thought . . . with Crystal out of the picture, maybe . . ."

"Cut it out, Al. And don't go putting ideas in Marilyn's head, either. Got it?"

"Got it," I said.

o-O-O-o

Elizabeth and Pamela both came over the next day to help me put on my bridesmaid's dress and specially dyed shoes to match, and the string of fake pearls and the earrings.

"I'll powder your back," said Elizabeth after I'd put on the slip and strapless bra.

"Powder my *back?*" I said. "Why?"

"So it doesn't shine," she said. "Women are always supposed to powder themselves when they wear backless dresses so their skin doesn't shine."

I don't know where Elizabeth gets this stuff. Her mother *looks* normal enough. "Elizabeth, tell me," I said. "I really want to know. What's wrong with a shiny back?"

Even Pamela had never heard that one.

"It shows she's perspiring," said Elizabeth.

"So?"

"So she's sweating! Women aren't supposed to sweat."

I guessed it would be breathing, next.

"Elizabeth, *everyone* sweats. What do you suppose our bodies do when we play volleyball? Leak?"

"Well, in the Olden Days," Elizabeth informed us, "they referred to it as 'glowing.' If a woman sweat, it meant she did manual labor, and if she did manual labor, she was no lady."

"We've come a long way, baby!" said Pamela, and we laughed, even Elizabeth.

Nevertheless, my back was powdered, my fingernails polished, my hair curled, my eyebrows plucked, my makeup applied, my panty hose untwisted, and finally the beautiful jade green gown was slipped over my head. I looked like Cinderella. Dad took a picture.

Patrick rode over on his bike to see me off, and I felt as though I was the one getting married. I realized I was the first one of our crowd to be a bridesmaid, and we all knew this was a big step into the adult world.

"What's this Danny guy like?" Patrick asked as he held the car door open for me and waited while I got the hem of my dress inside.

"Nice. High school senior. He wants to go into engineering," I said.

"He make any moves on you?"

Why is it that when a guy asks about love, it sounds like wrestling or something?

"He was a gentleman," I said.

"Good," said Patrick.

Dad and I got to the church a half hour early, and then everyone stood around and waited for the bride. They say that brides are always late for their own weddings, but when it became fifteen minutes past the hour, then twenty, I began to get nervous.

What if Lester wasn't home studying at all? What if he and Crystal had this secret plan to elope at the last minute? Wouldn't that be wild?

Standing at the back of the sanctuary, I could see people looking at their watches now and then, or turning around to see if Crystal had come. Even Peter wandered into the foyer asking us if anyone had seen Crystal.

I realized I still wanted something outrageous to happen—if not to me, then to someone else. I wanted it to be something a lot more profound than dyeing my hair green. There were too many unresolved things in my life: Dad and Miss Summers; Janice Sherman without either a boyfriend or a uterus; Patrick acting dumb; Mark acting worse; Pamela's parents separating; Elizabeth refusing to go out alone with Justin Collier, who was obviously wild about her. Me . . . *Every*thing about me was up in the air.

I wanted action! Decisions! I wanted, as Les might say, an event to change the course of human destiny, mine in particular. I wanted chapters to close, so that others could open up, and I could get *on* with it!

And then, just as I was prepared for anything, I heard whispers from downstairs. Crystal was coming up with her maid of honor holding her train. She looked as happy and excited as any other bride on her wedding day, and if she was thinking at all of Lester, you sure couldn't tell it.

The music changed suddenly to something louder and more grand, and people sat up expectantly. A door opened on one side of the altar, and Peter came in with his best man. Then the ushers joined them. Peter stood with his hands folded in front of him, half turned so that he could see the back of the sanctuary. All the men were wearing tuxedos.

The bridesmaids lined up in the proper order, and I swallowed. I wasn't sure if I was the bridesmaid who went first because I was the one who knew Crystal the least or because I was the shortest, but I didn't mind. Listening for my cue, I started slowly down the aisle. I couldn't help smiling, especially when I saw Dad smiling at me from one of the side pews.

The hard part was standing on one foot for a second before moving the other foot up. That little pause where you hope you don't fall over sideways.

Peter smiled at me, though, and everyone else was looking in my direction. I knew that once I got to the altar, the other bridesmaids would be halfway down, and then the maid of honor, so I just let my beautiful dress rustle as I walked, and let my beautiful toes peek out of my beautiful open-toed shoes, and let my beautiful hands hold my beautiful bouquet, smiling my beautiful smile.

I moved on over to the far end of the altar, across from the groomsmen, and turned so I was half facing the congregation. The other bridesmaids were on their way, and finally Crystal appeared in the doorway, holding her father's arm.

The music changed again, bolder still, and everybody stood up. I almost expected the organist to play "God Save the Queen." I wonder why people do that at weddings—stand up for the bride? As though she's more important than the groom. When people are standing, no one can see her, anyway.

But finally Crystal got to the front of the church, her dad kissed her cheek and let go of her arm, then everyone sat down again except the wedding party, and the ceremony began.

I realized suddenly that my eyes had filled with tears. No! I didn't want to cry! I didn't want my mascara to run. But the ceremony was so solemn and beautiful, I couldn't help it. What I wanted, I guess, was for it to be Lester standing up here in front of the church with his friends. *Lester* looking at Crystal the way Peter was looking at her, and for both of them to live happily ever after. I gulped and swallowed, and when I could, I slipped one hand to my face and quickly wiped my eyes.

And then I saw Lester standing at the back of the church, to one side of the doorway. My heart almost stopped. He hadn't received an invitation, but he'd come anyway.

Yes! Do something outrageous, Lester! I pleaded silently. Charge down the aisle, swoop Crystal up in your arms with her petticoats rustling and her satin shoes pointed toward the ceiling! I wanted her to say, "Oh, Lester, I *hoped* you'd come!" and Lester to say, "I can't live without you. Sorry, Pete!"

Now, Lester, *now!* I begged with my eyes. I didn't want my life to go on undecided the way it had. I wanted Lester married now! I wanted Dad engaged! I wanted to know if I would really become a psychiatrist, and I wanted all my friends to get their heads on straight.

I must have been staring so hard at Lester that the bridesmaid beside me noticed, because she gave a little nudge. I concentrated on the minister again, but when I glanced toward the back of the church a moment later, Lester was gone. The minister asked if anyone knew of any reason Crystal and Peter should not marry, and no one said a word. Les had just wanted to close a chapter in his own life, that was all.

By the time I heard the words, "I now pronounce you man and wife; Peter, you may kiss your bride," I was weeping again, and when the wedding procession went back up the aisle, and I put my arm in Danny's, he fished a tissue out of his pocket and handed it to me.

Everyone else got to go to the hotel where the reception was being held, but the wedding party had to stay at the church longer to have their photographs taken.

I decided one thing: I never want to be an actress or model. I absolutely cannot stand to wait and wait and wait. For people to be ready. For the photographer to be ready. For lining up and checking heights and straightening collars and arranging dresses. When the photographer snapped our pictures at last, my smile felt as though it had been carved into my face with a penknife, and my jaw ached from looking pleasant.

At last we were done, and we drove to the reception. We entered couple by couple until finally the bride and groom were announced. The band began to play, and Crystal and Peter danced slowly around the floor, their eyes on each other, the spotlight on them. Then the bride danced with her father, the groom danced with his mother, and I was glad when all the obligatory dancing was over because it meant we could eat.

Dad had found some people he knew to sit with, but I sat at the head table beside Danny, with the wedding party. There were lots of toasts to the bride and groom, and every time people started clapping rhythmically, Crystal and Peter were supposed to stop eating and kiss each other. Finally they didn't pay attention to the clapping anymore and just ate.

Dad said I could have a sip of champagne to toast the bridal couple, but no more. There was a bar, though, and a table full of beer on ice, and I noticed that Danny had a couple of beers.

It's strange, but as I was sitting there at the head table looking out over the room, I began to feel that my life *was* moving forward—that at last I was growing up, because I realized how foolish it would have been if Lester had run off with Crystal. She'd made her decision with no guarantees whatsoever, and Les and I had to do the same. Maybe Lester wouldn't marry anyone. Maybe I'd change my mind and decide not to be a psychiatrist after all, but at least I was inching closer to the person I wanted to be—more than just a clone of everyone else, but not so outrageously different that I had to wear green spikes on my head.

I had just taken a bite of my scalloped potatoes when Danny said, "Come on, let's dance." Other people were out on the floor, so I wiped my mouth and got up.

Please help me remember how to slow-dance! I prayed, and wondered if God paid attention to a girl who seemed to pray most when she was in a tight spot.

As soon as Danny put his arms around me, I could smell the beer. I really hate the smell of it. But it was Crystal's wedding, after all, and I decided I'd be a good sport. I put one hand on Danny's shoulder. Instead of holding my other hand out to one side, though, Danny held it between us, at chest level, so he was sort of pressing his hand against my breast.

He smiled at me through half-closed eyes, and kept pulling me closer. We stayed at the edge of the crowd, out of the spotlight, and moved back and forth from one foot to the other, but it seemed we were hardly moving at all. It made me uncomfortable. I suppose it was flattering in a way that Danny was so attracted to me, but how did I know it was me that was doing this to him and not the beer?

He leaned forward and nuzzled my face, then licked my ear, moaning a little. I tried to pull away and laugh it off, but he just pressed closer against me. Our bodies were so close already, I felt like a grilled cheese sandwich. I thought of all the times in seventh grade I had watched the beautiful eighth graders kissing by their lockers, their bodies glued to each other, and how I had envied them.

But suddenly I didn't want Danny's beer breath in my face. I didn't want his tongue in my ear and his hand pushing down on the small of my back.

"Danny . . ." I said.

"Shhhh," he whispered lazily, and moved me slowly around the floor.

"I'd like to go back and finish my dinner," I said.

"You can always eat. It'll wait," he said.

"Please stop it."

"Stop what?"

"What you're doing."

He moaned again. "What am I doing?"

The music stopped, but Danny didn't let go. He kept moving me around the edge of the dance floor, and we were still locked together, like two dogs in an alley. It was embarrassing.

The music began again. It wasn't a song I recognized, but the ONE, two, three, ONE, two, three were familiar.

And suddenly I pushed myself away from Danny, removing his fingers from my back, and walked over to Dad.

"It's a waltz," I said, and smiled.

I didn't even see what happened to Danny. Dad and I moved around the dance floor, the fastest couple there, taking this big first step, and then two little catch-up steps. ONE, two, three, ONE, two, three . . . Around and around we whirled. We were really traveling, and a few couples moved back to make room.

I just smiled and smiled. I couldn't help it. Dad was smiling, too. He looked at me as though I were a princess, and for that one night I was.

Crystal may have married the wrong man, and Patrick might never grow up, and who knew what would happen to Pamela, Elizabeth, and Sylvia Summers. But right at that moment, on the day after Thanksgiving, I was doing a waltz with my father, and we made quite a couple. Outrageous, in fact!